Double Action

When the drifting gambler, Luke Hackman, rides into Cameron City, Arizona, he finds himself in a heap of trouble. Four Mexicans have been savagely murdered and there is immediately an explosion of violence.

The despotic Brad Cameron and his gang of thugs rule the town, but, in Luke, Brad sees a man who bears an uncanny resemblance to himself and will perhaps provide the answer to his prayers. The Feds are on his trail and he needs to disappear, so why not kill Luke and bury his past?

He assigns murderous Pi-Ute 'breed', The Hunter, to do the job and Luke rides for his life as bullets whistle through the canyons bordering the Grand Canyon. But Luke still faces many uncertainties. Can he turn the tables? Can The Hunter become the Hunted? Can the amiable gambler fight back? Who will help him break Cameron's thraldom? And can he kill his mirror image . . . ?

As the death toll rises the good, the bad and the beautiful fight for their very survival.

Double Action

Jackson Davis

A Black Horse Western

ROBERT HALE · LONDON

ISBN 0 7090 7399 2

Robert Hale Limited
Clerkenwell House
Clerkenwell Green
London EC1R 0HT

Typeset by
Derek Doyle & Associates, Liverpool.
Printed and bound in Great Britain by
Antony Rowe Limited, Wiltshire

ONE

Arsenio Chavez sat in the shade of an oak occasionally giving a flick of his whip at a *burro* that plodded round and round, turning a wheel to divert their stream into artificial channels to water the crops. Not a cloud in the blue sky doming over them. A day like any other in the fifty years he and his extended family had lived in this valley, and, probably the generations, too, of their ancestors, going peacefully about their lives in spite of marauding Apaches, the lash of the Spanish conquerors, and more recently, the coming of the *Americanos.*

He watched his wife, Esther, and daughter, Isabella, bent double, their rumps in their long skirts thrust high as they planted rows of corn in the soggy fertile ground. Women's work. He would give them a hand soon: go and change the flow of the channels. Water. It gave them all life. A pleasant, peaceful scene. The children were at school in Cameron learning to speak American, to read and

5

write, things Arsenio knew little of. But, otherwise, nothing much changed. His sons were out in the hills tending to their small herd of cattle, sheep and goats. . . .

Suddenly a muffled explosion in the distance made the chubby-jowled Chavez jump from his reverie. What the hell was that? Esther and Isabella, too, rose from their labours, alarm on their dark features, listening. Another roar of an explosion barrelled along the valley towards them. And another.

'It's the Camerons,' Esther screamed at her husband. 'What are they doing?'

Isabella, still slim even after bearing three children, unlike her well-fed parents, sniffed at the air like an animal. 'That isn't gunfire.'

'They're dynamiting!' Her father shouted in Spanish. '*Madre de Dios*! What next?'

All had been well in this quiet northern corner of what was now termed Arizona Territory until the man called Cameron had arrived, naming the town after himself, opening a saloon and gaming hall, a bank, general store and real estate office. He had begun buying up all the fertile small *ranchos*, like theirs, roundabout. He had, indeed, offered them a good price to move out. But, how could they? Where would they go?

Arsenio began walking back towards the flat-roofed, adobe farm houses and outbuildings he and his family shared. But, he paused, removing his sombrero, wiping the sweat from his brow. It was too hot. High noon. The burning lozenge of sun

6

creating a humid one hundred degree heat. He returned to sit in the shade. 'What are they up to?' he muttered, darkly. 'We will find out soon enough.'

His wife and daughter returned to their task in their lush, fertile allotment. But, within an hour, as they were preparing to go back to the house to eat and siesta, something terrible happened. The worst thing possible. Their stream slowed to a trickle and the water wheel grated to a halt. The *burro* looked around, as perplexed as his owners, then licked at the sliver of water fast disappearing into the mud. Where had the water gone?

There were angry shouts from the house as Arsenio's two sons, Demetrio and Ronaldo, came riding in on their mules to the courtyard. 'They have dammed the river,' one shouted. 'There is no water for the stock.'

The family members, even the ancient grandmother, Rosa, who presided over the kitchen, stared at each other, fear and apprehension in their eyes. 'Without water,' Rosa hissed, 'we will all die.'

Arsenio clambered on to the back of a *burro*. '*Andalé.* Let's go see what's going on.'

They followed their valley as fast as their animals' legs would go until they arrived at a great wall of tumbled rocks. The father and two sons stood on the damp sand of their dried-up river bed and stared upwards. 'Holy Mother of God,' Arsenio whispered. 'What have these hyenas done to us?'

'Let's climb up,' Ronaldo suggested, but as he

jumped up on to the first rock there was the crack of a rifle shot and a bullet whined past his head chipping fragments from another rock into Demetrio's face. They jumped back, startled, and peered upwards as a man stepped out on top of the unnatural dam, his shape silhouetted dark against the sky. He wore a high-crowned black Stetson, a poncho thrown back over one shoulder, a Winchester .44-40 rifle hugged into his shoulder and aimed at them.

'The Hunter!' Demetrio's throat contracted at the sight of the half-breed Pi-Ute who roamed the hills shooting game for sale in the town and worked for Cameron as his main bodyguard. He was renowned as a deadly shot. 'What,' Demetrio croaked out, 'have you done with our river?'

For answer the 'breed squeezed out another of the bullets, the largest available on the market, and it whipped off Demetrio's straw hat. He jumped back from the rock looking around for cover. The Chavez men froze in their tracks as the sound of the shot echoed away along the valley.

'The river is not yours,' The Hunter shouted down to them. 'It belong to Señor Cameron now. You try to climb up here I kill you. You are tres-passers.'

'This is not fair, ' Arsenio shouted back. 'You know this is our water. It has been ours for years.'

The Hunter shrugged. 'Pah! This is not your land. It belong to Apache. Now it is Cameron's. This' – he jerked the Winchester at them – 'decides whose water it is.'

'But,' Ronaldo cried, 'we cannot live without water. All our stock will die.'

'So, go sort it out with Cameron.' The Hunter raised his rifle and his teeth flashed in a sneer. 'Or go live someplace else.'

The sun was westering fast, sinking behind the mountains beyond the rim of the great canyon, staining the sky above Cameron blood-red as the Chavez men slowly rode into town. They wore the white pyjama-like costumes of most *peons*, their feet in rope-soled *huaraches*, straw sombreros shading their eyes. The father, Arsenio, held his only weapon, a double-barrelled Parker shotgun in one hand, which he usually used only to defend his chickens from marauding foxes and coyotes. Ronaldo had a slim-barrelled hunting rifle, a .32, tucked in the cinch of his mule's saddle. Demetrio was armed only with a working machete that hung from his saddle horn. They were followed on foot by four of their women-folk.

Slowly they rode down the wide, dusty main street watched by a scattering of folk about their business in the town. They were mostly Anglos, who paused in the shadow of the sidewalks, or in the act of loading buggies with grain, aware that there was trouble in the air.

The Chavez clan reined in before the two-storey brick-built, Cameron bank. Arsenio climbed down and stepped across the dirt and up to the locked double-doors. He hammered on the brass knocker. There was no response. He shook his head and returned to his sons. He took a stand before his *burro* and looked up at the double windows above the bank. 'Señor Cameron,' he shouted, 'we want to talk, to you. What are you, a coward, ashamed of what you have done? We come in peace, Señor Cameron, we just want to talk.'

Suddenly, the double windows above the bank front door were thrown open and a burly six-footer, Brad Cameron, stepped out on to the stone balcony. In a dark, sober suit, he appeared to be unarmed. He scowled down at them. 'What do you greasers want?'

'You know what we want,' Ronaldo shouted, angrily. 'You have dammed our river. You had better blow up those rocks and give us back our water, pronto, or else.'

'Or else what?' Cameron growled, chewing on a cigar. 'Have you come here to threaten me?'

'Leave this to me,' Arsenio chided his sons, holding his shotgun pointed at the ground, and called up to the banker, 'Have pity, *señor*. You know we cannot live without water. This is not lawful. Why do you do this to us? We have not harmed you.'

'It's my water. I got first right. You got any complaints you better speak to my lawyer. Come back in the morning. We're closed for today.' Cameron grinned at them and turned as if about to go back inside.

'You lousy stinking gringo,' Demetrio hollered, unhitching his machete and waving it in the air. 'You stay and talk to us now. We want that dam blasted back down. Tonight, you hear?'

Cameron turned back and glanced down at him. 'What did you call me?' He looked across to the saloon where his barkeep, Steve Fellowes, had stepped out through the batwing doors. He had a Colt Thunderer double-action revolver gripped in his hand. 'Steve, tell these no-good trash to get back to their rathole.' He waved his cigar, distastefully, at the group below.

'We go nowhere 'til we get some answers.' Ronaldo jumped from his mule and pulled his hunting rifle from the cinch. 'You come down here, Cameron.'

For reply Cameron raised his cigar towards a man crouched on the roof of the meat market forty yards off, taking cover behind the false front sign of a painted steer. The Hunter squinted down his sights and squeezed the trigger of his rifle. As the explosion cracked out the heavy bullet smashed through Arsenio's head as if it were a water melon, killing him instantly.

Splattered with blood and bone, Ronaldo stared with horror at his father's headless corpse, and turned to seek out his assassin, raising his own rifle and thumbing the hammer. But craftily, The Hunter had the setting sun at his back, dazzling the man below. He squeezed the Winchester's trigger once more and the slug powered through Ronaldo's chest and out the other side. The young Mexican spun in his tracks, blood gouting from his front and his back, as he toppled into the dust.

Demetrio wheeled his mule around and raced

him towards the barkeep Fellowes, his razor-sharp machete raised. The 'keep looked alarmed, backed away, and fired his revolver wildly. The third bullet took out the young Latino and he went spinning into the dust. Fellowes ran across and emptied his cylinder's last three bullets into his back to make sure.

The Chavez women were screaming in panic. The wizened Esther ran to kneel beside her husband's headless torso. She snatched up his shotgun and raised it to fire at Cameron. The 'breed had slid another slug into the Winchester's breech. As Esther sent pellets flying and Cameron jumped back to avoid the blast, The Hunter fired. His bullet knocked the woman off her feet and she lay dying in the dirt, her blood draining from her. 'Go,' she choked out to Isabella. 'Go quick before they kill us all.'

But Cameron, a tad shaken, had stepped back out on to his balcony. He raised his cigar to the half-Apache. 'That's enough. You women go get your brats from the school and clear out. The undertaker'll take care of them dead of yourn. You can bury 'em tomorrow. Let this be a lesson to you. Nobody argues with Brad Cameron.'

He watched Isabella and her brothers' wives down on their knees wailing and moaning over the gunned-down kin. 'Go on, get out! Quit that cater-waulin' or I'll kill you all.'

As the tearful women rose and straggled away, Cameron was about to go inside, but he turned to the onlookers, standing like statues in the sun's afterglow, their eyes condemning him. 'What's the matter with you?' he roared out. 'You saw what happened. Them greasers attacked me. It was self-defence. A fair fight. Go on, get back to your homes.'

TWO

'Cameron City,' the rough-cut sign said. 'Pop. 304.' The latter number had been recently crossed out to read, '300'. Luke Hackman hauled in his horse and pursed his lips, considering this information. 'Sounds like they've had four sudden deaths,' he muttered.

He nudged the sturdy skewbald onwards along the bank of the fast-flowing Little Colorado River towards the collection of adobes and plank houses, his first sign of human habitation in fifty dusty miles. 'Maybe we'll see what pickings we can take here tonight, eh, hoss, an' mosey on tomorrow.'

Hackman was a Texan, a big, deep-chested young man who needed a big horse to carry his weight. The powerful skewbald stood all of seventeen hands, unusual in a land where most men rode scrawny mustangs or cow ponies. What few folks were around turned to watch him as he sauntered in along the wide main street of baked mud between a collection of false-fronted stores. 'Cameron and Co., dry goods and grain'; a gunshop, restaurant, ladies' clothes place, meat mart, dairy produce; the Cameron stage line and livery; the customary collection of enterprises until he came to a two-storey brick building on his left, the Cameron Bank, and opposite it another high, double-floored edifice, the Golden Eagle saloon.

Luke swung down from his high-prowed saddle and tied the reins of the horse to the hitching rail. He removed his Stetson and leather gloves and ran fingers through his flaxen hair, which immediately sprang back to hang across his brow. He stroked the five days' growth on his solid chin and slapped the dust of five nights sleeping rough from his mackinaw. In his sun-bleached, high-heeled boots, his fringed buckskin chaps over faded Levi Strauss jeans, his blue, cross-over canvas shirt, silk bandanna and gunbelt, he looked the epitome of a prairie drifter. An amiable man, mostly, he was astute enough to realize that his sort were not welcomed with open arms in small 'cities' like this one. He glanced through narrowed eyelids at a clutch of hard-looking *hombres* in range clothes who stood in the shade of the sidewalk watching him. He replaced his low-crowned Stetson and climbed the steps to the saloon entrance, pushing through the batwing doors and pausing for a few moments while his eyes became accustomed to the gloom.

'Yeah?' The barkeep was polishing glasses and at this early hour of the morning the saloon was practically deserted. 'You want somethang?'

'Yeah, something to cut the dust from my throat,'

15

Hackman drawled. 'Gimme one of them Prickly Ash beers you got advertised outside.'

He strolled through the card tables, passed a roulette table, with a swing of his hips, touching a finger to his hat to a girl who sat at a bar stool. Luke was polite to ladies, unless they proved not to be a lady and he was giving this one the benefit of the doubt. He was kind to animals, too, well kinder than most men in these parts of Arizona who merely regarded a bronco as a work tool to be whipped into submission. Sure, he had been known to smash his fist into a nag's jaw if it tried to bite him, but that was just to show it who was boss. It generally had the desired effect and they got along fine after that. He stood with his powerful shoulders hunched, his hands resting on the top of the mahogany bar, and licked his dry lips with anticipation as he watched the beer trickle from the tap into the glass.

'Don't tell me,' he said. 'Let me guess. Who owns this classy joint? Cameron?'

'That's right.' The 'keep cut foam from the beer with a spatula, dropped in a chunk of ice, and sent the glass sliding along the bar top to his waiting hand. 'Why?'

'No reason.' Hackman shrugged and took a long draught of the ale. 'Just surmising that maybe he owns most the damn town.'

'Maybe he does, but what's it to do with you, mister?' The barkeep was wearing a collarless shirt, with garters around the sleeves. 'If I were you I'd keep remarks about Mr Cameron to yourself. We don't take kindly to nosy characters in this town. Nor, come to that, to drifting prairie rats, neither. They are generally advised to move on along.'

Luke grinned, his cheek dimpling, his grey eyes twinkling. His heavy eyelids drooped as he snorted his mirth. He had a deceptively sleepy air, rather like a man who had been smoking the happy weed. It had fooled many an opponent before now. 'That what you think I am?'

'That's what you look like, mister, a lowdown, panhandling bum.'

'Don't be misled by appearances.' The stranger studied his empty glass then slid it back to the 'keep. 'Gimme another, creep. You know, just for that crack I've a mind to stay here tonight and clean up this fair city.'

'You got cash to pay for this?' When Hackman spun a golden eagle worth twenty dollars the barkeep quickly snatched it, tested it with his teeth and put it into the drawer of an ornate cash register. 'What you mean, clean up?'

'I mean first I'm gonna clean myself up, get a bath and a shave, then I'm gonna come back and clean up at that roulette wheel. Thass what I am, a gambling man.'

'Oh, yeah?' The 'keep slid back his recharged glass with a sneer. 'Well, you just better be careful what you're doin', mister, 'cause folks round here don't take kindly to any sneaky underhand professional tricks.'

'Seems to me like they don't take kindly to a good many things. I ain't allowed to talk about the boss

17

man. I got to mind my manners. How about you, lady?' Luke turned to let his lazy gaze wander over the girl. 'Whadda you say?'

The girl, or more of a woman now he looked closely, was sitting on a barstool, her slim figure encased in a tight dress of blue satin, with a collar of white lace. Her dark hair was drawn back into a bun. In some ways she looked highly respectable, but her rouged and powdered face, the way she smoked her cigarette and shrugged, offhandedly, gave him some doubts.

'It's nothing to do with me, 'she said, 'but it might be advisable to heed Steve's words. Card cheats get a sticky reception around here.'

'Would those four fresh graves I counted as I passed the boneyard just now have any bearing on that remark?'

'You mind your own business,' Steve Fellowes shouted. 'Those lousy greasers gave us trouble and deserved all they got.'

'You don't say?' Luke winked at the woman, conspiratorially. 'What would you be, lady, the local schoolteacher taking her morning pick-me-up?'

The woman eyed the remains of a glass of bourbon, picked it up and tossed it down her throat with a grimace. 'Why, are you buying?'

'Why not? He seems to have pocketed my change.' Luke grinned as the barman strolled along and filled her glass from a bottle. 'But, just for your information, I don't deal a crooked pack. Or keep anything up my sleeves.' He opened his palms to them. 'I play by the rules.'

The 'keep combed back his brilliantined hair, peering into the mirror behind the shelves. 'In that case, stranger, how you planning to clean up?'

'How? Because,' Hackman drawled after taking another deep sup of beer, 'I stay off the whiskey and I play better than most of the dumb hicks I encounter. Fair enough?'

'That might be interesting to see.' The 'keep slid him back ten silver dollars in change. 'The action generally starts about five in the afternoon and goes on to five in the morning. We'll see just how good you are. It'll be a pleasure to see you skinned.'

'Who spins the wheel?'

'Me.' The girl gave a peel of laughter. 'Why? You wanna start now?'

'You?' Luke looked at her with surprised amusement. 'You know I had a silly idea you might have a different profession.'

Her painted lips broke into a bright smile. 'Maybe for a fella like you I could combine the two. You interested in parting with that ten dollars?'

The gambler regarded her crossed legs beneath the long, tight skirt, her white-stockinged ankle, the high-heeled slipper dangling as she gently swung one dainty foot. 'Kinda pricey, aincha, in this place?'

'If you don't like it go drink someplace else,' Fellowes snarled. 'The next saloon's forty miles on along the trail.'

Luke stood in his dusty mackinaw, the butt of his Remington revolver jutting out from his hip. He let the ten silver dollars clink from one hand into the other, then pocketed them. 'I guess I'll wait to see how my luck is. Maybe I'll be able to buy us a magnum of champagne.' He met her eyes and smiled at her. 'What's your name?'

'Ruby. What's yours?'

'Luke. Luke Hackman. Ruby, eh? That kinda sounds right. To tell the truth, Ruby, I don't generally have to pay my wimmin. They do it for free.'

He turned on his heel and sauntered out, pushing through the swing doors.

'Cheapskate, ain't he?' Steve Fellowes raised his voice so the stranger might hear. 'Who's he think he is?'

'We'll see. Is it a bluff? Or can he really shoot the cards?' Ruby extinguished her cigarette in a glass ashtray. 'One thing's for sure, he ain't having me for free.'

'You notice somethang funny about him, gal? He reminded me in some ways of the boss. When he first stood there at the door with the light behind him . . . the same big build, the same colour hair, same style. But, of course, I soon saw he was just some down-at-heel drifter.'

'You know, Steve, now you mention it, you're right. But that guy's got a different attitude. He's far more casual and relaxed than Brad. 'Ruby glanced rather wistfully out of the batwing doors. 'Yes, casual could be that fella's middle name. We'll see what he looks like when he's had a bath It might be interesting.'

'Why the hell you in such a funk, Sheriff?' In his

office above the saloon Brad Cameron sat in his leather swivel chair behind his desk and roared the question out at a fat perspiring man with a tin star on his shirt who stood before him like a carpeted schoolboy. 'I tell you those greasers pulled their guns on us. We shot 'em down. It was as simple as that. Fair fight. Why all these questions?'

'Because, Mr Cameron, I ain't planning on being charged as an accessory to homicide. Folks are saying those Mexicans were harmless. And killing the woman was unnecessary. They came to see you with a legitimate grievance. It's said you and your men shot them down in cold blood.'

'Sure, they came to me with some kind of grievance, trying to make out that I had cut off the water to their land. Are you calling me a liar, Finnegan? Two of them had guns, and the other one pulled out a machete. My men would swear to that. The woman picked up the shotgun and tried to kill me. What folks are these who are talking? Point them out to me. I'll soon put them right. I bet they're just a bunch of dirt-poor farmers. Who pays any account to them? Why are you so het up, Sheriff? This ain't like you.'

Cameron poured coffee from a silver pot and added cream. It was true, in build he was very similar to the dusty drifter who had just slaked his thirst downstairs, a man he had yet to meet. He had the wide shoulders, the massive chest, the same six-foot height. His hair, too, was flaxen in colour, parted to one side, with the same unruly habit of falling over his brow. But he lacked the fellow's amiable smile and laughter lines. Brad Cameron was rarely amiable to anyone. He didn't have the time. He was hitting thirty and he believed a man should have made his fortune by that age if he was going to. Sure, he had plenty of property, land and cash stashed away, but to be secure he needed more.

Sheriff Hank Finnegan watched Cameron trim the end of a cigar and lick it with his lips. Hank fumbled for a match in his waistcoat pocket, leaning forward to offer a light. When Cameron sat back and blew out a smoke ring, Hank tossed the match away and, with some hesitation, ventured, 'I shouldn't be telling you this, Mr Cameron. It's what they call classified information I've been issued on you.'

'Just what the hell are you talking about?'

'The federals. I've been told to hold you pending their arrival. Really, I oughta put you in the lock-up.'

'Federal agents?' Cameron's eyes widened with shock and fear and the blood seemed to drain from his face. 'Coming here?'

'That's what they say.' The sheriff was surprised to see Cameron looking so rattled. He had thought him a man immune to fear. 'Coming to arrest you for something you did back East. They say you were involved in the forgery of currency. That's why it's a federal offence. That's why I can't turn a blind eye to this gunning down of the Mexicans. I gotta show them I'm doing my job. Like they say, I oughta hold you.'

'Just you try it, Hank.'

'No, I ain't gonna do that. You been good to me, Mr Cameron. But you must see the position I'm in.

We oughta have an inquest, a proper inquiry into those deaths.'

'Shee-it!' Cameron suddenly stood up and hurled the coffee pot at the wall. 'Federals. I thought I'd given them the slip. I thought they'd never find me in this out-of-the-way hole.'

'Maybe,' the sheriff prompted, ' I could arrest you and you could break out of jail.'

'Listen, you tub of lard, I ain't interested in covering your arse. Nobody's putting me in jail.'

'Sounds like they're gonna have a damn good try.'

Cameron chomped on his cigar, angrily. 'It's no good me running. Those vultures will keep on my trail. I got to disappear, take on a new identity. It's got to look to them like I'm dead. That's the only way they'll close the case.'

'How you gonna do that?'

'There are ways.' Cameron patted the sheriff's shoulder. 'Thanks for warning me, Hank. You do as I tell you and you'll be OK. There'll be a big pay-off for you. All you gotta do is keep your mouth shut.'

Cameron paced across to the window and stared out of it down at the dusty main street. 'I gotta think of something. How long have I got?'

'Not long. They said they were on their way.'

'How to fool them? That's the question.' Cameron gave a start when he saw Luke Hackman stroll from the livery stable. 'Hey, come here, Hank. That big guy, who is he?'

'Hell knows. I never seen him before.'

'Wouldn't you say he looks a tad like me?'

'Hey, yeah. That's strange. If he was better dressed

he could be your dead ringer.'

'Dead's the right word. Go see what he's doin' here, Hank. Don't let him leave town even if you have to arrest him.'

THREE

To a fanfare from the shotgun's bugle and in a cloud of dust the six-horse stage from Flagstaff came rolling in. 'Whoa-ay-yaugh!' the driver roared as he hauled the rig into a halt in front of the Golden Eagle saloon.

The shotgun threw a strongbox down to a waiting clerk of the Cameron Bank. The driver clambered down to throw open the coach door. 'Here y'are, folks. Overnight stay in Cameron City. We'll be on our way at first light.'

A portly drummer, in his stovepipe hat and check suit, was the first to step down toting a carpet bag of patent medicines and household samples. 'Whoo!' he cried. 'What a ride! I know a tarmacadam surface like back in Tennessee might be out of the question, but hasn't anybody heard of filling in the potholes on these trails?'

'Aw, quit whining,' the stage guard growled. 'You easterners are all alike.'

'I might remind you to show a little more respect

to your customers, my man. It is we who pay your wages.'

The drummer gave a squawk as the guard booted him up his plump backside and shouted, 'Git out of it. Go an' peddle your wares.'

Two other passengers tumbled out. A curly-haired young man in a four-button city suit and bow-tie grinned at the drummer's expostulations as he gave his hand to a girl in a dove-grey travelling costume. 'Here we are, honey. The Golden Eagle Casino. I've heard of this place. There's gambling all night.'

'Aw, no, Billy. You promised you wouldn't.' The slim girl, of about nineteen years, straightened her little pillbox hat and veil. 'You promised. Not tonight.'

'Don't worry, Sal. I'll only play a coupla hands. I've booked us the best room in this joint. We ain't gonna waste the use of a big feather bed, are we? It'll make a change to your ole man's barn. You go an' tidy up and I'll be having a drink at the bar.'

A blush rose to the soft cheek of the girl as her consort referred in such a loud voice to their previous courting ground and activities a modest young lady did not boast about. Billy could be very brash at times.

The driver winked at a small crowd of onlookers as the young couple went inside and he picked up their baggage to follow. 'Newly-weds,' he said. 'They're on their honeymoon.'

Luke Hackman smiled with the rest of them as he stroked his newly-shaven chin and hitched up the pants of the grey tweed suit he had paid $2 for at

Cameron's clothing emporium. He was wearing it with a blue wool shirt and a loose-fitting dark-blue bandanna. You could say blue and grey were his favourite colours. They certainly heightened the twinkling grey of his eyes as he turned to glance at the setting sun. It was 5 p.m. Time for his business day to commence.

He had had a ride around the small, so-called city – well, any collection of bank, saloon and subsidiary buildings was generally called a city in the West – and found a widow lady in a white-painted cottage along the way who took in lodgers and had a lean-to for his horse. She had cooked him a steak, with apple pie and cream to follow, and he had taken a long nap, catching up on his sleep, in the cool of her back bedroom while she washed his shirt and jeans and put them out to dry. She was a nice lady, Mrs McKenzie, one of the best. You wouldn't find better for a dollar a night.

'OK,' he drawled, as he took a stance by the roulette table and Ruby strolled over to join him. 'How about we give it a whirl.'

'Ain't you drinkin'?'

'Not while I play, no. Gimme ten dollars-worth of chips.'

Roulette wasn't really his game. The odds against winning were not good. Thirty-six to one, with the added zero and double-zero for a man to buck. However, he generally managed to hold his own while he waited for a poker school or something to start. He could hear the honeymoon kid at the bar laughing and making puerile jokes with a couple of local barflies who were glad to let him pay the rounds. 'Sounds like he's getting a bellyfull of the juice.'

'Yeah,' Ruby said, as she used the scoop to shove some chips back his way. 'I kinda feel sorry for that young wife of his. Place your bet. You still on the red?'

'Sure, I seem to be doin' better than I thought.'

'Well, you're all duded-up. Maybe it's making you smart.' Ruby gave him a secretive smile. 'Keep playing. It could be your lucky night.'

'You don't say? Some fat-gutted sheriff cornered me just now and told me I'd better not try to leave town, so I may as well enjoy myself while I'm still around.'

'Yeah, you might as well, mister, 'cause you ain't got long to be around.' Brad Cameron, in a room above the casino, was watching him through an opaque spyhole glass cut into the floor. 'That's the way, Ruby, keep him sweet. I got plans for this bozo.'

Down below Luke Hackman watched the ivory ball bounce around the spinning wheel until it trickled to its slot allotted by fate, or, in this case by Ruby Hendrix's toe as she operated the brake on the wheel hidden by the table canopy. With expert manipulation she could generally make sure who won or lost.

'Red twenny,' she sang out. 'Hey, stranger, you're on a winning streak.'

'Yeah, funny, ain't it?' Luke stacked his chips. 'I think I'll give it a break while I'm on the lucky side.'

'Hey, don't back out now.' Billy, the newly-wed, had lurched over to join him. He slapped his shoulder and tossed a five-dollar bill down for chips. 'You might just pass on some of that luck of yourn.'

Luke made a quizzical, down-turned grimace. 'I doubt it, son. If I were you I'd give this table a miss. Why doncha go up and see that li'l beaut of a wife of yours. She'll be waiting for you.'

'Aw, I got all night for that. This is the action I'm looking for.'

'Look, son, you oughta take some good advice while you're still sober.' Luke placed his hand on the youngster's shoulder. 'Don't play. This ain't gonna be your night.'

'How the hell do you know?' Billy brushed him off, wildly. 'What's it got to do with you?'

Ruby cooed, 'Place your bets, gen'lemen.'

'I know because you ain't sober enough to play. That juice they been shootin' you is their local moonshine. It could kill a mule.'

'I can take my whiskey.' Billy bet on the red twenty, too, as the wheel began to turn. 'What you think I am – some snotty schoolkid? Just who you think you're talkin' to?'

'You ain't got a chance.'

'Who says?'

'Look!' Luke watched the kid lose. He wanted to tell him that the table was fixed, but even that wouldn't stop him. He knew that. He'd got the gambling fever. And anyway, the fix had been good to him. If he'd lost it might have been a different matter. Maybe Ruby had the hots for him? Or, maybe, there was something more sinister? Why should the house want some drifting stranger in town to win? Billy was pulling out a wad of dollars, peeling off four fives, gambling more desperately.

'Ach. Forget it. Where do I cash in my chips?' Luke asked.

'Over at the desk.' Ruby smiled, her eyes inviting. 'You were right. You are cleaning us out. How about that magnum of champagne you were talking about and us celebrating later.'

Luke twitched a lip at her and turned away. 'It wouldn't taste right.'

A hundred dollars he had won. A cow-puncher's wages for four months. Maybe he would have one drink. 'Gimme a glass of bourbon, not that crap you call whiskey. Yeah' – he stubbed a finger at a bottle on the higher shelf – 'the stuff the man upstairs drinks. Why do I have a feelin' he's watchin' me?'

'You're crazy.' The 'keep, Steve, had put on a clean celluloid collar and lashes of brilliantine for the evening. 'Why should he be interested in a cardsharp bum like you?'

'That's what I'd like to know.'

Luke Hackman paid for his drink and sauntered over to a table in the corner, taking a chair with his back to the wall. He savoured the tumbler of bourbon. Yeah, it was the real McCoy. The last of the sun's rays were filtering through the saloon's batwing doors as a boy went around lighting whale oil lamps. His thoughts drifted back to the days before he had learned to respect this stuff. When he, too, had been a damn fool drunk, throwing away everything he had

30

on the last roll of a dice, whoring, fighting, destroying his marriage, and for some reason destroying the love of his life. It was a long while ago. He had been drifting since she walked out on him. From small town to small town. From Texas up to Montana and Wyoming, back through Colorado, to New Mexico, and up through Arizona. Trouble seemed to follow him, but, at least, he figured, he had learned a little more horse sense.

Suddenly the girl, Sal, she was called, appeared on the landing and looked down at her young husband as he wildly threw away their money on the roulette table. She shook her head, sadly, and descended the stairs to the casino. She had changed into a virginal white cotton dress, with gold trimming, and brushed her blonde hair until it shone. She wore an opal gem on a black velvet choker around her throat and when she reached the floor looked the picture of hesitant innocence among the raucous men drinking at the bar, or huddled around the roulette table, watching the greenhorn losing his dough.

'If I had a gal like that I wouldn't be wasting my time at the table,' Luke muttered. 'At least, not these days.'

He watched the girl pluck up courage to push through the throng to reach her husband. Eventually they appeared to argue. She tugged at his sleeve. He thrust her angrily away. The girl withdrew and looked about her, seemingly at a loss.

'Hey,' Luke called, getting to his feet. 'Would you care to join me, miss? Fancy a drink? Don't look so scared. I won't try to whisk you off.'

'I . . . I . . . yes, a sarsaparilla, if I may?'

When they were settled down, he clinked glasses and asked her, 'Where you two heading?'

'Well . . . we were going north to take a look at the Grand Canyon. They say its an awesome sight. We're supposed to leave at dawn. But when Billy gets on a spat like this I don't know if I'll be able to drag him away.'

'Yeah, don't I know the feeling?'

'Why, are you a drinker and gambler, too?'

'I used to be a drinker. I'm just a gambler now. You can't mix the two. Not if you need to make your living by it.'

'You mean you're a professional?'

'Cardsharp? Go on, say it. You sound disapproving.'

'Well, how do you win? Surely you must have to cheat?'

'Nope. I don't need to. I'm good at my job. And suckers like your husband just give me their money. Look at him. It's like taking candy from a baby.'

'It's not candy. It's a lot of money. It's the money my father gave us to set up home. Billy vowed he'd taken the pledge.'

'To give up the booze and the cards? It ain't as easy as that. I know.'

'But you.' She looked disapprovingly at him. 'You've no other compunction than to fleece people. You take their money without a care what happens to them.'

'Young lady, don't moralize me.' Luke took another taste of the bourbon. 'More fool them. It's

32

my job. Mind you, some can get mighty disagreeable about it sometimes. The odds against staying alive ain't high if you're a gambling man.'

'Oh, dear.' Sally bit her lip, distractedly, as she watched her husband leave the roulette game and lurch unsteadily over to the bar. 'I don't know what I'm going to do about him. He gets out of control when he's like this.'

Billy had weaved his way over to them, another whiskey in his hand, a sneer on his face, his curly hair hanging over his brow. 'So, you've found yourself a friend? What's he telling you, that I ain't got a chance in hell? Well, we'll see about that. I'm joining this blackjack game, Sal. I'd rather you went up to our room and waited for me. Won't be long. Soon as I win back my losses I'll quit. Go on. I don't want you talking to this guy.'

'There's nothing like that,' the girl replied. 'This gentleman's just being kind.'

'Yeah, a likely story.'

'Don't you realize how boring it is, Billy, just sitting around watching you play these stupid games? Surely I can talk to somebody?'

'Go to bed, Sal. Thass an order.' Billy was slurring his words and swaying, somewhat. 'I'll be up soon.'

'I had better go,' Sally murmured to Luke. 'I don't want a scene.'

Luke got to his feet as he bade her goodnight. He turned to her husband. 'I think I'll join you in that game.'

The man called The Hunter had strolled in, laid his

rifle aside and joined the game, the dark planes of his face impassive, his eyes in their slits contemptuous as he assessed Luke across the table. By four in the morning the dawn's light began to lighten the casino. Beneath a canopy of cigar and whale oil smoke four players remained in the game. The drummer, in his Lincoln hat and loud-check suit, had lost some cash but was chubbily cheerful. Like all Indians, The Hunter loved gambling and played doggedly on even though he, too, had had a bad night. Billy looked frazzled for practically all the cash he had possessed was now piled up in silver cartwheels and notes on the table before Luke. The Texan had removed his jacket which was slung over his chair back, and he studied his hand with cool nonchalance.

'Waal, whadda ya know,' he drawled. 'It seems to be my lucky night.'

'Yes,' the salesman agreed, 'the gods have smiled sweetly on you, but not on us.'

'There's something fishy about the way you keep winning,' Billy sneered. 'That deck's had so much dodgy dealing it's dog-eared.'

The Hunter's cruel lips broke into a taunting grin. 'Those are dangerous words, sunshine.'

'Well,' Billy cried, 'how the hell did he win that last trick?'

There were a lot of unspoken rules about blackjack and people played a lot of systems, but the object was to beat the dealer, who happened to be Ruby. She, too, was as cool as a cucumber, sitting there in her satin dress, her hair now piled up on top and clasped by a diamante brooch.

'I can open another new pack of cards if you wish, sir,' she said, 'but you better accept the fact that the most skilled person wins at this game and not come out with cruddy remarks like that.'

'Look, kid,' Luke said, with a sigh, 'I don't usually reveal my expertise to amateurs, but I'll tell you where you went wrong there. I had a real weak seven of diamonds while you had a nine of hearts and nine of clubs. You split your cards and increased your stakes. That was a fool thing to do.'

'Oh, yeah, why so?'

'My advice to you would have been to stand. You had a strong eighteen. My most likely draw would have been a ten or a picture. You would have had an automatic win.'

'Now he tells me.' Billy groaned and put his head in his hands. 'OK.' He pushed one of his few remaining dollars across. 'Deal me in, sister. I'll try again.'

They played again and The Hunter gave a whoop of glee as for once he won. He had drawn an ace and a queen which equalled blackjack. 'I'm gittin' lucky.' His green eyes were filled with contempt as they met Luke's. 'Watch yourself, mister.'

'I'm not cutting any more capers,' the drummer remarked in his flowery manner. 'Defunctness is odiferous.'

'What's he talking about?' Billy muttered.

'I mean I'm out of this, as you ought to be. Sweet Morphia beckons me. I have patent medicines to sell in an hour or three.'

Ruby flipped out the cards again as Billy rolled

another dollar across. He had a four of diamonds and five of hearts and, according to received wisdom, doubled. Again he lost. 'Hell,' he groaned. 'What went wrong that time?'

'Look, sonny, I'm not here to teach you to suck eggs. You should have known Mr Hackman's two of hearts was dangerous. You took an unnecessary risk doubling. You still in, sir?'

'Yeah.' Billy raked his hair out of his wild-looking eyes. 'I'm near enough broke. Makes no difference now. Might as well go and throw myself off the rim of the old Grand Canyon.'

'Damn fool,' Luke remarked. 'Don't say I didn't warn you. What's that purty li'l wife of yourn goin' to say?'

'I dunno.' Billy appeared to be in abject despair as he knocked back his whiskey. 'Guess she'll divorce me. Thass the end of my honeymoon.'

'Waal, I've had enough,' Luke drawled, scooping in his winnings and filling his coat pockets. 'Sorry to discombobulate you gentlemen, as the drummer might say, but it's the land of nod for me, too.'

'With you gone I might stand a chance.'

The Hunter grinned. 'Not against me and Ruby. But try your luck, kid.' He scratched at his muscular, bronzed neck and chest in the open shirt. 'Go on, I dare ya.'

Luke got to his feet, pulling on his jacket and tipping his Stetson over his brow. He tossed a ten-dollar bill to the woman. 'So long, Ruby. Thanks for the deal. Or was it a double deal?'

He grinned at her, glanced at the barkeep, Steve,

who was lounged in a chair nearby, watching through narrowed eyes, and sauntered out into the early dawn.

Down the street the stagecoach driver and his shotgun were backing their six-horse team and harnessing them. It would soon be time for the honeymooners to head forty miles on to see the great gulf of the big canyon, but how could they now?

'Aw, hail,' he muttered, clawing fingers through the pile of dollars in his pockets, about three hundred and fifty in all. There was no one else around. At the side of the saloon was a staircase leading to a veranda at the front of the building. He climbed up it and trod as silently as he could along the creaking boards. He peered into the window of a bedroom. The drummer was snoring like a pig. No. There was a wider window, probably the main double bedroom, its window open for the breeze. He drew the curtains aside and saw Sally peacefully sleeping, her honey-blonde hair spread across the pillow. He climbed deftly inside and went across to sink down beside her, putting his hand over her mouth as she gasped awake with surprise.

Luke met her eyes and shook his head, negatively. 'I'm gonna take my hand away. Don't make a sound, Sal.'

'No, please, don't do this.' There was fear in her eyes. 'My husband will kill you.'

'He could try. It ain't what you think, gal, although I can't say I would be adverse to your charms. You look real tasty.'

'What do you want?'

'That damn fool husband of yours has gambled away everything you own. Why did you marry that idiot?'

'I – I had to. I'm carrying his child.'

'That's reason enough, I guess. But, look, here's two hundred dollars.' He began laying the cash out on the coverlet. 'I'll keep the coin and give you the notes. It'll be easier for you to conceal. You hang on to it and you pay the bills from now on. Tell him it's a reserve your daddy gave you and he's not to have it.'

'You mustn't do this,' she protested, 'it's yours.'

'Aw, easy come, easy go. Quick, stick it in your bag. Anyway I figure it weren't won fair. For some reason Ruby made sure I won. Maybe she fancies me. Come on, do as I say. He'll be up any minute. It's time for you to pay your hotel bill and catch that stage. You're on honeymoon, remember?' He pinched her cheek. 'Smile!'

Sally swung out of bed in her cotton nightdress, and started pressing the notes into her silver reticule. There was the sound of footsteps coming along the corridor, unsteadily, Billy groaning at his bad head and bad luck. Her lustrous eyes met Luke's as he backed away to the window. 'Why are you doing this?'

'Waal, let's just say I once knew a gal like you. I treated her bad, just like Billy's treating you. Maybe it's conscience money.' The gambler touched his hat brim to her, and exited through the window. The girl blinked tears from her blue eyes, then hid her bag under the pillow as her husband stumbled through the door.

'Aw, Sal, I'm sorry,' he wailed. 'I lost the damn lot.'

'Never mind. Maybe it will be a lesson to you, Billy. Come on, I'll get dressed. You can sleep it off in the coach.'

FOUR

Luke Hackman was half-asleep on his feet as the
flush of dawn spread over Cameron City. He took a
short-cut through an alley which he believed would
bring him out by the widow's cottage boarding
house. He was fumbling to light a cigarette when a
big bruiser, masked by a bandanna, in range clothes,
stepped out before him and slugged him a straight
right to the jaw. 'Unh!' The gambler recoiled and as
he did so he was buffaloed across the back of the
neck by a revolver butt. He went down on his knees
but grabbed at the bruiser's waist, hauling him down
with him. He smashed his fist into his jaw in retalia-
tion, and turned on his back to kick his boot into the
other man's groin. He, too, was masked, and
groaned with pain as he spun his Colt and tried to
aim at Hackman. The gambler kicked out again
sending the Colt flying.

'Kill the bastard,' another man cried as he
stepped into the affray as Luke tried to get to his

feet. He thought he recognized one of the voices, the perfume of brilliantine, before the third man's boot slammed into his cheek toppling him back on to his first assailant. The latter grabbed him around the throat and began choking his life out. The Texan struggled desperately, but the constriction of his air pipe, the boots and revolver butts hammering into his head and belly, the thorough beating, finally told and he passed into unconsciousness.

'What the hell's he done with his winnings?' one of the mughunters asked as they roughly searched him. 'There's only a hundred and fifty here. Look in his boots. It must be someplace.'

A store clerk on his way to work was shaking him by the shoulder when Luke Hackman came to. 'Are you all right, mister?'

The gambler shook his head and painfully raised himself. 'Waal, I'm still alive, that's something. But I guess they skinned me. I walked right into it.'

The little man helped him to his feet and opined, 'You ought to see a medic. Some mess they made of your face.'

'Thass all right. I'm OK.' Luke swayed and had to grab for the wall to support himself as his head spun. 'Thanks, anyway.'

He stumbled on his way down the alley, gasping at the sharp pain in his side. Maybe they had caved in a rib or two? He wiped blood from his nose and mouth, jerked at his teeth. They were still intact. One eye was half-closed but he could still see. He concentrated on getting back to the widow's.

'Gawd!' she squawked. 'What's happened to you?'

'I got jumped for my cash,'he mumbled through his swollen lips. 'There was three of 'em. Don't you worry now.'

When he looked in her fly-specked kitchen mirror as he washed his face in a bowl of water he saw his eye and lips were puffed up, an egg-shaped blue lump was on one cheek and his shirt was crusted with dried blood. The widow hovered around him dabbing at his wounds with lint.

'You better lie down, 'she said. 'I'll go for Doc Blount.'

'No. I got an idea who did this. If you could jest bile me up a cup of black cawfee, thass all I need.'

At least they had not robbed him of his long-barrelled Remington revolver. He pulled it from its scabbard, spun the cylinder and checked its load. Six trusty friends still in there. He thrust it back, angrily, and sat on a stool in the kitchen sipping at the scalding brew.

'Right, I'm fine now,' he said. 'Maybe I'll be back for a late breakfast. Maybe I won't. We'll see how the dice rolls.'

He left the widow's clapboard house and headed back to the Golden Eagle casino, occasionally pausing to clutch at his ribs as the pain and nausea hit him. 'Some coyote's gotta pay for this,' he muttered.

Steve Fellowes, minus his celluloid collar, but with bracelets around his sleeves, was cleaning the bartop and serving the first few early morning customers. It was 10 a.m.

He looked up, his eyes briefly meeting the Texan's as he pushed through the batwing doors, and quickly darting away towards two men sat at a table in a corner imbibing whiskey. 'Yeah,' he growled. 'Whadda ya want?'

Ruby, too, was on her bar stool, a whiskey-sour in her hand. When did she ever sleep? Luke wondered. 'Hi,' he called, nodding to her as he stood at the bar.

'What in hell happened to you?'

'I got run over by a stampede.'

'It sure looks like it.'

Luke rolled a hand across his swollen lips and gave the barman a direct look. 'You sure like to splash that brilliantine around. A man could smell you anywhere, even up a dark alley.'

'What you talking about?' Fellowes creamed the foam off a pint of beer and sent it sliding along to a gent further down the bar. Luke glanced at him. In a derby and suit he looked harmless. The others around were just carrot-pickers.

'This.' Luke reached out and caught Fellowes by a clump of his greasy hair, dragging him towards him and smashing his head down on the bar. 'It's payback time. Where's my dough?'

'Agh!' Fellowes came up, blood trickling from his eyes. He shouted an obscenity and tried to haul out a sawn-off twelve gauge. 'You—'

Luke grabbed the barrel and pushed it skywards as it blasted out lead pellets. He twisted it from

Steve Fellowes' grasp and hammered the stock into the barkeep's jaw. He went spinning back, crashing into bottles and glasses. He managed to right himself and stared into the long mirror behind the shelves.

'Yeah, take a good look at one dumb hick.'

In the mirror the Texan saw one of the two men in the corner stepping towards him pulling out a revolver, raising it to get a good shot at his back. Luke turned and blasted the second barrel of the shotgun at him, hitting him in the chest, knocking the man to the floor.

Ruby screamed. 'Look out, Luke!'

He followed the direction of her pointed finger and saw the second man in the saloon corner had grabbed at a carbine and was levering a slug into the breech, aiming from the hip. Lake hurled the shotgun at his head, making him miss his aim. The slug ploughed past his thigh into the mahogany woodwork of the bar. Luke's Remington was out in double-quick time and he fanned three bullets at the *hombre* making him spin in his tracks before toppling to the floor.

He turned to check Fellowes, shoving the Remington's eight-inch dangerous end up his nostril. 'Right, do you want the same treatment or are you giving back my cash?'

'OK, you win.' Fellowes' hands were trembling as he reached in his back pocket and pulled out a pouch of fifty silver dollars. 'We split it. They got the rest. Don't kill me. I stopped them killin' you.'

'Yeah, maybe that was your big mistake.'

'What in hell's going on?' Brad Cameron had burst out from his office and was standing at the top of the stairs, a rifle in his hands pointed at the Texan. 'Just hold it right there, stranger.'

'You're too late. These three robbed me of my winnings and then drew on me.' Luke turned to doff an open palm at the attendant ranch-hands and farm boys. 'Ain't that so?'

'Yeah,' one yelled. 'It was a fair fight. Them three pulled iron on the stranger first. He's lucky he's still alive.'

'Luck or judgement.' Luke went across and gave a groan of pain as he bent down to relieve the two bloody corpses of their ill-gotten gains. 'This big one's spent ten of my cash but I guess there ain't no point in suing him.'

Cameron, in his neat shirt and suit, came down the stairs and across to Fellowes. 'You idiot, I oughta have you strung up.'

'But, boss,' the 'keep stuttered, 'You—'

'Shut up.' Cameron slapped him a back-hander across the jaw. 'Get out. Go on, get outa my town.'

'You can't do this to me—'

'I'm doing it. Git on your hoss and vamoose. I don't need you around no more. Take your back wages from the till. That's five dollars. Now scram. This gentleman is a valued customer. We cannot have him being attacked when he leaves my establishment.'

'You never said,' Fellowes moaned, as he clutched his jaw, picked up his jacket and hobbled to the door. 'How was I to know?' At the swing doors he turned

45

and eyed them malevolently, his greasy hair hanging over his eyes. 'So, this is what I get for five years doin' your dirty work, Cameron? You ain't heard the last of me.'

'*Get out,*' Cameron roared, then turned and grinned at Luke Hackman. 'I guess the least I can do is buy you a whiskey. You look like you could do with one.'

'Make mine a drop of that bourbon,' Luke replied, as Cameron went behind the bar. He spun his revolver, blew down the barrel and stuffed it back in its leather holster. 'So, I guess you're the big man around these parts?'

'That's me.' Cameron put out a hand to shake, but Hackman ignored it. 'Welcome to Cameron City. Sorry about that bit of hassle. Those halfwits thought they could take you, huh?'

'Yeah, they learned otherwise.'

The saloon cook had poked his nose in to see what all the noise was about and his boss called to him. 'Charley, toss those stiffs outside 'fore they stink-up the place. They're bleeding all over my floorboards.'

'Made a dent in your bar, too.'

'Ach.' Cameron raised his glass to the Texan. 'That's nothing. I can assure you it don't happen often. This is a law-abiding city.'

'Goodness gracious!' The portly drummer was coming down the stairs, tying his bow tie. 'Can't a body get any sleep in this place?' He stared, wide-mouthed, as the corpses were dragged out by their boot-heels. 'My, my! What's been going on here? I've heard of the Wild West but this is extraneous.'

'Listen, mister,' Cameron bellowed, 'you wanna stay healthy you better go poke your nose in some-place else.'

'Tut. Tut. That's no way to speak to a paying guest. May I remind you I am a man of artistic constipation. Sheets and Kelley are my midnight companions. Not to mention the infamous Lord Tryon.'

Luke gave him a double-take. Was this joker seri-ous? 'How about Oscar Fingal O'Flaherty Wills Wilde? Hear tell he's making a tour of America.'

'Ah, yes,' the salesman squealed, 'Oscar and I are blood brothers. I adore his ladyfriend, Lily Pantry. There's a town named after her in Texas.'

'Langtry,' Luke corrected.

'Yeah, why don't you go an' join her,' Brad Cameron growled. 'Two pansies and a lily would look fine.'

'Ha! You jest. Cast pearls before swine. But while we have a little crowd here.' The drummer opened his carpet bag and produced a small bottle labelled 'Heroin'. 'Why not try some of this magic cough mixture? Related to morphine. Latest thing on the market, folks. Only two bits a bottle.'

Ruby slid from her stool and went over to take a peek. 'I'll try some. Might do my throat good.'

'I use it myself,' the salesman trilled. 'It embalms me with a curious sense of *véjà du.*'

Cameron turned his back on him. 'So, Hackman, you playing tonight? Gonna give the house a chance to recoup our losses? Doncha worry about these killings. Won't be no charges. I'll fix it with the sheriff.'

'Like you fix everythang around here?' Luke tucked away his $140 and sampled his bourbon. 'You know, I got a funny sensation I met you someplace before, mister.'

Brad Cameron studied his doppelgänger. 'Me, too. Odd, ain't it? You ever been in Kentucky? That's where I was raised. Opened my first saloon and gambling parlour in Memphis, Tennessee. You ever worked the river boats?'

'Pal, you name it, I've probably been there. N'Orleans, St Louis, Virginny City, Denver, Santa Fe, Silver City, New Mexico, Tombstone, Tooh-sohn, and here I am, points north, probably headed for Californ-nay-yay. We'll see. But my kin are back in Texas.'

'Looks like I'll be needing a new barkeep. How about helping me out 'til I find one.'

'No thanks. Ain't interested in barkeep's wages. I'll probably be movin' on in a coupla days.'

'Not before we win our money back, I hope.' Cameron patted his shoulder. 'Well, good luck to you, Hackman. My apologies, once more, for what happened to you. This is a fine town and we don't like to treat strangers that way.'

'You don't say? How about Mexicans?'

'Ha! A man with a sense of humour. Look, Luke, while you're here the bar's open to you. Ruby, anything this man wants you see he has. He's a valued customer. Be good to him. I must go. I got work to do over at the bank.'

'Sure, Brad. You did say *anything*?' She grinned at the big Texan as she wandered behind the bar, found a broom and swept up the broken glass. She took a gold-sealed bottle from a cooler. 'The boss said treat you right, so how about this? Best French bubbly. Ain't this what you promised me if you got lucky. It's on the house.'

'How about you? You on the house, too? Maybe you know some place comfortable where we could split this bottle?'

'My room's upstairs, cowboy.' She winked at him. 'But I can't promise you'll get much rest.'

When she closed the bedroom door Ruby turned to kiss him, her mouth sultry and moist, as he undid the eyelets on the back of her dress with expert fingers and caressed her silken skin.

'That's lovely, 'Ruby murmured as her dress rustled to the floor. 'Kiss me some more.'

'First things first.' He popped the cork of the champagne and filled two glasses, clinking his with hers. 'You know,' he said, as he sampled it, 'I cain't for the life of me figure out why everybody, apart from them three, is being so nice to me.'

'Oh,' she smiled, cupping her drink, stepping from the dress and kicking it away with a stockinged toe. 'Like Brad said, we're real friendly people in Cameron City. That Fellowes always was a trouble-maker. We're well rid of him.'

'Yeah? Seemed to me he thought the boss would have normally backed his little prank.'

'Oh, no,' she laughed, bouncing back on the bed and placing her glass on a sidetable. She lay back on the pillow in her silken bodice, in her cheap rhinestone necklace, bracelet, ring, and crotchless calico drawers, pouting her painted lips at him. 'We're not like that. Perish the thought. Come on, mister. How about some action?'

Luke unbuckled his gunbelt, slung it over the bedpost, sat and hauled off his boots. 'Jeez,' he groaned, 'it's been a long night. I gotta take it easy. Feel like I got a rib or two caved in.' He dropped his pants and rolled in upon her, laughter shimmering in his eyes. 'You know, Ruby, I can't figure you out. You seem too cute for this rathole. Too bright. Is there anything going on 'tween you and Cameron?'

'Well, a gal cain't say no to the boss, can she, not if she wants to keep her job. But it's nothing serious. Doncha worry your head about it.'

'I ain't worried,' Luke drawled, as he gripped her under her thighs and hoisted them aloft.

'Oh, gee,' she cried, 'are we into playing wheelbarrows?'

Brad Cameron stood at the window of the bank and looked across at the Golden Eagle saloon. Ruby had drawn the curtain across her bedroom window. 'Thass right, gal. You keep him sweet,' he muttered. 'We need this creep to stay in town a couple more days.'

He returned to his office safe, taking out various deeds and accounts. He would wind up all his assets in Cameron and put the strongbox containing all the cash he could raise, on the stage to Tucson. From there it was an easy step to the Mexican border. He would buy himself a big ranch, take over a new town. The Feds would have no authority down there. Brad Cameron was never beaten. Those fools had better think again if they had that idea.

FIVE

'Hi!' The drummer, Alphonse Strudl, smiled brightly as Luke descended the saloon stairs. 'You could doubtless do with a reviver after encouching with that hussy!'

'You taken the job as 'keep?'

'Only as a temporary interjection to my career. My cough mixture is not selling well. Let me make you one of my Manhattans.'

'Sure, I'll try anythang once.' Hackman sat on a bar stool and out of habit took a pack of cards from his pocket, shuffling and fanning the deck out on the bar top, face-down. 'Pick an ace.'

The drummer chose one and upturned a two of clubs. 'They're marked,' he chided as Luke produced an ace of diamonds.

'Nope. But I ain't telling you how it's done. You playing tonight? Hear tell a couple of big ranchers coming in for a poker game. They heard about me. Stakes should be high.'

'Not my game, dear boy.' Alphonse, in a pink shirt,

velvet cravat and gold-threaded waistcoat, filled two glasses half full of rye, syrup and bitters, and added vermouth. 'There, gargle that. Did you know it was invented in '45 by a New York barman for a wounded duellist?'

'You don't say, what's your handle – Alphonse?' Luke took a taste and smacked his lips. 'Mmm, not bad. You'll make a good 'keep, Alphonse.'

'Please, I'd prefer to be known as a dispenser of aperitifs. 'Keep! Such a vulgar appendage.'

'Well, I gotta buy me a clean shirt, git a shave at the barbershop and take me a bath.'

'Very wise, sir, if you've been mingling juices with that meat-mincing minx. Don't want a dose of Cupid's measles, do we?'

Charley the cook came in. 'Hey, fatso' – he prodded Alphonse in the gut – 'you better empty that spittoon before tonight.'

'Mercy!' Alphonse stared at the brass vessel almost overflowing from well-aimed baccy chaws. 'The emptying of foul cuspidors is definitely not my department. Nor can I be expected to man-handle fifty-gallon whiskey barrels. That is your superfluity. I will go protest this instance to Mr Cameron.'

Luke raised his eyes heavenwards as Alphonse flounced off out of the saloon. His bottom wobbled in his pinstriped pants as he waddled across the dirt street towards the bank. 'You've met your match there, pal.'

'The fat bastard, complain to the boss, would he?' Charley muttered, darkly. 'I'll piss in his soup, I will.'

Luke winced as he finished the Manhattan and

ambled towards the door. 'Yeah? Well, remind me to eat someplace else.'

The drummer strode into the bank, ignored the head cashier and climbed the stairs to the banker's office. The door was slightly ajar. He was about to push it open when he heard voices inside. So, he decided to knock, raising his knuckles, but paused. The conversation was not one to be arbitrarily interrupted.

'I want you to make a good job of it,' Brad Cameron was saying. 'It's got to be a headshot. Blow half his face away. Here, you take my wallet, my keys, these letters, my keyring I always carry, my gold watch and put them on him. You dispose of his revolver and put my pearl-handled Hopkins and Allen in its place. You let me know as soon as it's done then I'll give you my will, leaving the bank, the store and the saloon to you and Ruby. And I disappear under cover of darkness. The coroner will certify his death as mine. You can say it must have been a revenge killing by one of those Latinos. All you have to do then is pump some lead into the sheriff one of these nights. He blabs too much. And I hope I never see or hear from y'all ever again. I'll be changing my name and starting a new life. Any questions?'

'Nope. Fair enough.' The drummer recognized the deep, guttural voice of the half-Indian known as The Hunter, and peeped through the crack of the door to confirm this was so. The 'breed, in his high-crowned hat and fringed poncho was sprawled in a chair opposite the banker, one boot crooked up over his knee. 'Best of luck to you, Brad. You've allus treated me square.'

'You've always done a good job for me. I don't want to leave. We had a nice li'l set-up here. But it's a case of having to. The Feds are after me. So the sooner you get this done the better it will be. I figure if we rook him at the poker game tonight he'll be ready to move on tomorrow. All you have to do is follow him a couple of miles and then strike. In the meantime I'll make a pretence of riding out in full view of everybody and wait for you at the cabin. Is that clear?'

'Couldn't be clearer, Brad. It's a cinch.'

Alphonse lowered his knuckled fist and retreated quietly down the stairs. 'I think I will empty that cuspidor after all,' he muttered. 'Really! What on earth will happen next?'

When The Hunter had gone Brad Cameron called his chief clerk, Cy Cooper, up to his office. 'I wanna make a codicil to my will, Cy.'

'Thought you were leaving the saloon, etcetera, to the 'breed and Ruby.'

'You joking? No, I'm leaving it all to my nephew, Hiram McGinty, Jr., care of the bank at Nogales, Mexico. You got my new identity documents ready yet?'

'Fresh off the press, buddy.' Cooper produced a birth certificate, bank draft and other items. 'I ain't lost the old touch, have I?'

'Excellent.' Cameron gave a whistle of awe as he admired what Cooper had achieved on his small printing press out in the back shed. 'You always were too damn good, Cy. That's how they caught us. The government couldn't make dollar notes as good as yours.'

'Those were the days back in Memphis, eh, Brad? I won't be sorry to get out of this desert country. Our talents are wasted here. We should do OK down in Nogales. It's a border town, smuggling, gambling, prostitution, numerous illicit enterprises we can move in on, Brad.'

'Call me Hiram from hereon. Hiram McGinty, Jr. Yeah, it's got a good ring. Nope, I'm going legit from now on. I plan on putting all our assets into a big ranch and a silver mine down in Durango. You'll get your share, of course. We been together a long time. A couple of Federal lawmen ain't gonna stop us now.'

'When you reckon they gonna arrive?'

'Anytime, if they're lucky. I'm arranging a reception committee. Then as soon as our friend the gambler is a gonner I'll clear out and head for the border. You join me as soon as you've seen through "my" burial and the new will. Don't forget to order me a nice gravestone.'

'Hang on a minute.' The former forger was a neat, balding man with a trim moustache, of slight physique. He had always let Cameron call the shots, but now he hesitated. 'Why should I wait behind? The Feds will be after me, too.'

'I doubt that, Cy. I'm the one they want. You've always kept low profile. If you're worried give yourself a new identity.'

'I already have. I'm Jorge Corillas, a Mexican

56

national, and I want half this will making out to me. It's not that I don't trust you, Brad, but I gotta protect myself, too. All we got to do once we've made this codicil is put it in the hands of that dumb hick lawyer, Harris, down the road. He'll see it through. I'm getting out the same time as you, Mr Cameron, or should I say McGinty? We stick together on this.'

'All you gotta do is hang around a couple of days. Otherwise it's gonna look suspicious you disappearing before they've buried me. All you gotta do is see things through, Cy.'

'No. It's too risky. I ain't waiting to be nabbed. I'll draw up this codicil and then I'm out.' The dapper little forger picked up the relevant papers about to return to his desk. 'Oh, by the by, did that roly-poly drummer, Alphonse, find you?'

'Alphonse? No, he's over at the saloon.'

'No, he came in the bank just now, about four, and went up these stairs to see you.'

'About four? That's when The Hunter was here. Alphonse certainly didn't come in here. Say, you don't suppose he overheard anything?'

'Who knows? He certainly left in a hurry.'

'Yeah? We better keep on eye on the fat boy.'

'Perhaps,' Cooper suggested, his eyes glinting behind his spectacles, 'you should add him to The Hunter's hit-list?'

They were poker-faced, the two men who rode in from their outlying ranches to play the gambler who in one night of blackjack had made quite a reputation for himself. Well, they would see how he aquitted himself at a real game. And he wouldn't be getting any help from Ruby this time.

They introduced themselves amiably enough. One, McKenna, was a tall, lean man, with a saw-toothed drawl, who kept his felt Stetson on the whole night and chomped on a cigar. The other, Harrison, in range clothes, had a hard face as weather-beaten as saddle leather. They weren't giving anything away.

Sheriff Hank Finnegan sat in for a while, perspiring visibly as he tried to suss out the game and saw his weekly wage fast disappearing into the pot. Before midnight he groaned and got to his feet. 'You gents are too nifty for me. I gotta throw in my hand otherwise I'll have to go pawn my Colt.'

'You don't want to do that, Sheriff, you might be needing it.' Brad Cameron guffawed as he studied his own hand.

'Anyone for Manhattans?' Alphonse called out as he went across, tray in hand, to collect the empty glasses.

'Just give me another drop of tarantula juice,' Harrison growled. 'You can keep your fancy concoctions.'

'Suit yourself, ducky.' Alphonse minced back to his bar. 'Some people!'

Ruby, too, had retired from the game. The stakes were too high for her. She sat on a bar stool, smoked a cigarette, and swung one leg, languidly, in her long satin skirt revealing a neat, stockinged ankle. A good gambler had to know how much he could lose. How high, she wondered, would Luke Hackman be prepared to go? These three were out to skin him.

'Give us something to shoot for,' McKenna drawled. 'You've got the best hand.'

'All right, twenty more,' Hackman replied, unruffled.

In poker you need to judge the psychology of an opponent. But there wasn't a lot the Texan needed to know about these three. They were rich, ruthless and expert players. It was going to be a matter of bluff.

By 3 a.m. Hackman had lost most of his first flurry of winnings. He glanced at his opponents in the low light of the flickering lamps. They were like a circle of wolves waiting to close in on him, their eyes cold and avaricious. Maybe he had bitten off more than he could chew? They had suckered him into this. He got to his feet, scraping his hair from his eyes.

'You quittin'?' Harrison asked.

'Nope. Jest going for a leak.'

'Right, gentlemen,' Cameron said, stretching, 'maybe it's time for a break?'

When he went through the kitchen to the back door Alphonse was dozing on a chair. He came to his senses with a start, and gawped around him. 'Is it over?'

'No, not by a long chalk.'

Luke was glad to step outside and get some fresh air, standing there, urinating against the wall, staring up at the bright stars. 'They're almost as big as those in Texas,' he drawled as Alphonse slipped out to join him.

The drummer sidled up too close for comfort and began to undo his flies, too. 'Hsst!' he hissed.

'Beware the tides of March, or in this case July.'

'Yeah?' Luke had read a little Shakespeare. 'You mean ides, doncha?'

'They plan to rusticate your head,' the drummer whispered as he piddled.

'What?'

'Send you heavenwards. In plain terms, kill you. When you leave this fair city 'twould be best you watched your back.'

'You don't say?'

'I do say. They plan to appropriate your corpse for illegitimate reasons. Don't say I haven't warned you.'

'Well, thanks.' Luke buttoned up and prepared to return to the game. 'So, let me give *you* a piece of advice. Don't eat the soup.'

Alphonse plucked at his jacket. 'Don't trust the ruby-hued cocotte. She's in it, too.'

Luke shrugged him off and Alphonse was left to scold himself. 'Now look what I've done. Gone all over my shoes.'

By 6 a.m. it was all over. 'You've cleaned me out, gents. Don't know how you done it, Harrison, but the pot's all yourn.' Luke rose to pull on his jacket and gave a wry grimace. 'You've taught me a lesson I won't forget. I ain't fool enough to hock my hoss and gun. Thass all I got. I'll be moseying on.'

'Sure.' Harrison's face broke into a grin for the first time as he scraped the pile of dollars into his corner. 'You put up a good fight, Hackman, but you ain't in our league. No hard feelings, I hope.'

'No, why should there be?'

He stuck out his broad chest and ambled towards

the door. Ruby slipped off her bar stool and put an arm around his waist, halting him. 'No need to go just yet. Aren't you coming up for a bit, darling?'

'I ain't your stud bull, lady.'

'You'll get my prize rosette.' She smiled up at him. 'Yesterday you loved me.'

'Yesterday was yesterday. Today's today. Times change.' He took her chin between thumb and forefinger and gave her a quick, rough kiss. 'So long, sweetheart. No man likes to be a loser. I'll try my luck along the trail a bit.'

'Luke, please.' Ruby hung on to him, tenaciously. 'I must tell you something.' She lowered her voice and whispered, 'Brad needs a double. You're the patsy. Get out, but go fast. The Hunter will be after you.'

'Why is everybody so concerned about my health?'

'I want you alive, Luke. You and I, we would make a good team.'

Luke looked around him, his heart pounding in spite of his outward calm. If what she said was true it might be best to leave under cover of darkness, eat up some miles along the trail, get a good start. He would need to be alert so he needed some sleep.

'Maybe,' he said, putting his arm around her own waist, 'I'll accept that invitation and earn my rosette.'

Cameron scowled as he watched them climb the stairs arm in arm to Ruby's room, slam shut the door. 'What the hell's she playing at? If she thinks she can two-time me. . . .'

'What's wrong?' Mckenna asked.

'Nothing.' Cameron shrugged and grinned. 'But the sooner that no-good, card-sharping bum gets outa my town the better I'll like it.'

SIX

The Hunter rode his mustang into town at about four in the afternoon, a four-pronger buck hanging limply across the horse's back-quarters. When he wasn't killing men, his main job was provisioning the Cameron citizens with game. The green eyes inherited from his drunken, worthless, Irish father, flickered in the slits of lids of his dark, implacable face as he raked the windows of the buildings for any signs of life. He was always alert for trouble. He had enemies, he knew, who might one day strike back, if they dared.

However, the town appeared peaceful. A good many of the citizens were just arousing themselves from their post-prandial *siesta* ready to return to the business of the day. Old customs died hard and most kept Spanish hours, especially in the summer when after noon the temperature could soar to 120 degrees on Gabriel Fahrenheit's register.

The Hunter held no allegiance to any of the region's three factions. There were the white Americans who were settling, trade and industry

63

revived since Geronimo and his Apache warriors had surrendered and were kicking their heels in Florida dungeons. The Latinos, their land surrendered by General Santa Ana after the Mexican war, had become second-class citizens. And, definitely third class, were the Indians, the Havasupai and Navajo, who were herded on to nearby reservations bordering the great canyon. The Hunter regarded them all with arrogant contempt. He was his own man, one of life's loners.

What had he in common with his Pi-Ute mother who had abandoned her tribe to live with the bullying braggart who had taken her as his squaw? Fortunately, a mining accident had resulted in the Irishman's demise or his bastard son might have hastened him on his way with his knife. Perhaps he had inherited the man's murderous, crafty temper, and the innate hunting skills of the Pi-Utes, a thieving, lying tribe who had made a living during the frontier conflicts supplying the Apaches with rifles and ammunition. Whatever, he was not a man to be trifled with. When he lithely dismounted from his mustang and stepped up on to the sidewalk outside the bank, Cameron's bunch of hard men hanging about in the shade of the canopy outside were not slow to move aside to let him pass.

He climbed the stairs to Cameron's office and shoved inside without knocking. He kowtowed to no man. 'I been waiting at Chimney Rock all damn day to back-shoot him but there ain't no sign of him,' he announced.

'That's 'cause he's still in the hotel. He's been

humpin' Ruby and I reckon she's given him an inkling of what's going to happen to him.' Cameron looked up from his books. 'Fer Chris'sakes keep your voice down. Don't tell the whole goddam town.'

'Ach! Who cares?' The Hunter's razor-thin lips made a down-turned grimace. 'Cowering over at the saloon, is he? Must be shit-scared of showing his face. He can't hide behind a woman's skirts for ever.'

'It's just as well you've come back. We only had his word for it that he was taking the trail north. If he knows we're out to get him he might change his mind and go south. All you gotta do is keep watch, then follow him out. But make sure he's well clear of town before you strike. Otherwise the plan remains the same.'

The Hunter helped himself to a handful of Cameron's good cigars from a fumidor on his desk, lit one up, stuck the rest in his vest pocket, and snarled, 'I know what to do. There's no way he can get away from me.'

Glancing at him Cameron could well believe it. The Hunter, in his trail-dust clothes, the clinking Spanish spurs, the six-gun slung on his hip, the *rebozo* draped back across one shoulder, and the black hat shading his eyes, had an air of menace about him. 'I hope so. We can't afford any mistakes.'

The 'breed left the bank, hefted the deer on his shoulder over to the meat market, had a meal of *frijoles* and *enchiladas* in a Mex dive and went to keep watch opposite the hotel. Towards sundown he saw the Texan stroll out of the saloon doors, jerk his hatbrim down against the fierce rays, and walk over to the store to make a few purchases: bullets, beans, both coffee and pinto, flour, baking soda, and a couple of cans of bully beef. The Hunter was bitterly amused to see that he carried, apart from his Remington revolver, only a Sharps' carbine. A single shot. He would be easy meat.

In the saddle boot of his mustang the 'breed carried his fifteen-shot Winchester rifle, the frame and butt-plate made of imported Sheffield steel, each of its .44 centre-fire cartridges propelled by forty grains of powder. Improved in 1881 it was the finest and deadliest weapon as yet produced. With The Hunter's knowledge of the local terrain, the Texan would not only be out-gunned but out-manouevred, too. He didn't have a chance.

The 'breed followed him on foot at a discreet distance and saw him enter the widow woman's cottage. He emerged a short while later, dressed once more in mackinaw, shirt, jeans and shotgun chaps. He went round the back to collect his horse, a magnificent, muscled animal. There the gambler did have an advantage, but a bullet through its forequarters would soon bring it down. However, The Hunter hoped that wouldn't be necessary for he had designs on keeping the big skewbald for himself.

From the cover of an ancient cottonwood tree he watched the Texan mount up, collect his reins, touch a finger to his hat to the widow who had come out to stand beside her white paling fence, and head off at a spirited gait. He was taking the northern trail. All The Hunter had to do was close his trap. He had nothing against the gambler. He just saw him as his target, the prey to be killed.

It was dusk and the 'breed hurried back to the centre of town to unhitch his mustang. He swung aboard, nodded to Cameron who was watching from out front of The Golden Eagle and cantered out of town by way of its backpaths, keeping in the shadows, as inconspicuously as he could.

Luke Hackman rode at a hard lope giving the skew-bald its head along the dust-white ribbon of trail that climbed and fell following the Little Colorado river. The moon had yet to rise but the stars glimmered in a clear sky. He had no idea where he was going. He had never travelled this way before. He had, of course, heard of the great canyons that split these lands, the Grand Canyon of the Colorado and the equally deep lateral canyons of the Cataract and the Colorado *Chiquito*. But the journals of the day were keen to describe the wondrousness of America's fertile regions as blandishments to incoming settlers, and rarely lingered on the desolation of the great desert areas. So Luke had little idea that he was entering an area that to some seemed like the end of the earth. He had a naïve idea that he could some-how climb down the cliff-side by mule trail and manage to cross this natural barrier, make his escape, reach California. So he urged his steed on, eager to get a good rifle-distance away from the man he knew would be following him. He was guided in his general direction by The Dipper star.

'Hot damn, ' Luke groaned as he saw the *Chiquito*, or

Little Colorado, enter a sheer-sided canyon, its mael-strom of water bubbling onwards in a sheer force of nature that over the millennia had cut its path through the solid rock. The trail he had been follow-ing had brought him out on to the top of the cliff edge. There was no way he was getting down there. Or, if he did, he would need a raft to float away along the meandering tumult of white water. And trees were not in abundance in these parts. By the light of the waning moon casting its silvery glow he could tell he was in a tract of stark, inter-cutting cliff ranges not unsimilar, he imagined, to the surface of the moon. The only sound of life was the mournful howl of a coyote. No wonder they howled!

He cursed his stupidity for lingering in Cameron City. He should have known by the sight of those four fresh graves as he rode in it was not a place to hang about. He cursed, too, his arrogance in thinking that he could add to his winnings from the Golden Eagle. Those two ranchers had sucked him dry, not for big stakes, but just to see if they *could* do. Even now his pride convinced him that they had played a crooked game, either through that spyhole in the ceiling, or some signalling device which revealed his hand. Whatever, they had cleaned him out like a baby, and left him with only a few dollars to pay for his horse's feed.

The skewbald had eaten up the miles through the night and now, as dawn's glimmer appeared in the east, he was obviously tiring. They must have come twelve leagues, or more. It was time to give him a rest, feed him some split-corn, for there was no natural grazing to be seen in this tortured land. 'Here y'are, fella,' he said, as he slid down from his high back, loosened his cinch. 'We gotta keep you going. You're my lifeline out of this.'

He looked around him, tried to figure out where the great stretches of rock were leading to, where he might find his way through. It looked as if to get out he would have to go back. There was no sign of pursuit, but that meant nothing. 'That bastard'll be sitting there waiting, laughing, knowing the terrain, smiling to himself, thinking he's got me hemmed in,' he muttered. 'Aw shee-it!'

He needed a rest, himself. It would be unwise to light a fire, give away his position, but, what the hell, the guy probably knew it anyhow. He took a swig of water from his canteen, but what he really thirsted for was a mug of hot black coffee. It was like a drug to him, concentrating his mind, giving him the energy to go on. He found some kindling, bits of dried sagebrush, yucca, and dead branches from a piñon bush that had somehow hung on to life in this inhospitable land. He got a small, hot blaze going and warmed his hands for he was stiff with the cold of the night. He could see he was gradually gaining altitude, or the river below was descending to sea level, he wasn't sure which. He crushed coffee beans with his revolver butt and tipped them in his enamel pot. Then he opened a can of bully beef and spread it with his knife on to a dry-tack biscuit. Hungrily, he clawed his way through this crunchy repast, and was leaning back against a rock sipping at the scalding coffee when a bullet sent splinters flying over him.

Luke powered himself across the fire, rolling for the cover of a rock as his horse gave a startled scream and plunged away. 'Hot damn, come back, durn you!' He gritted the words through his teeth as another blue whistler whirred past his ear. *Pa-dang!* It sent his coffee pot flying. The Texan peered through a crack in the rocks and saw an orange flash of flame, a puff of smoke, heard the explosions barrelling away through the canyons. The shootist was up on a ridge, almost a mile away.

'This fire was a mistake,' he muttered. 'I sure drawn a bad card. That joker's holding a pair of jacks with an ace kicker.'

If it was a Winchester, which he was pretty sure it was, the marksman would have thirteen more in the magazine and would be able to fire almost as rapidly as a Gatling gun. Luke cursed himself for giving his money away to the girl and losing the rest. He should have spent it on a hundred-dollar rifle like his opponent's. That way he would have stood a chance. His single shot Sharps carbine, while a trusty, accurate weapon, had a killing range of only two hundred yards at the most. It was no match in this situation.

Luke raised himself, gingerly, and searched around for the skewbald. He had charged off further down the slope, but, a well-trained beast, in response to his master's shrill whistle, had stopped and was staring dolefully back at him. Luke wondered why the gunman hadn't killed the horse. He was a big enough target. If he did he would be truly helpless.

He ducked back down as he heard the whine of another bullet and it almost took his head off, chipping the rocks and ricocheting away. It was too far a distance for him to make anything out of his assailant up on the ridge but if it was The Hunter, and he was pretty sure it was, he probably had the eyesight of an eagle. He was half-Indian, wasn't he?

Luke put two fingers to his mouth and gave another shrill whistle, but the horse remained where he was. 'The dumb critter's got more hoss-sense than to come back an' git shot at,' he muttered. 'Let's hope he stays where he is. It's a time to take chances.'

He gripped his Sharps in one hand and set off at a dash down the slope, leaping through the sand and rocks. There was the banshee screech of bullets snapping about him, but he zigzagged, changing course, and by some miracle evaded them. He took a flying leap from the top of a rock into his saddle, and, as the skewbald whirled, snatched up the reins, dragged the horse's head around and set off at a gallop for the protection of the nearest ravine. He was almost there when he felt his saddle slipping, and he remembered he had loosened the cinch. Slowly, inexorably, the saddle moved until Luke was hanging on to the horse's flanks almost under the pounding heels. He was forced to let go and was pitched bouncing and tumbling along the hard ground, the air punched out of him.

The skewbald went charging on its way into the safety of the high-walled coulée leaving its owner sprawled. The shooting had ceased. Possibly The Hunter had lost sight of him. Luke crawled back to retrieve his carbine, braced himself, and, keeping low, made another dash towards the ravine. He pressed himself to the shadow of the rock while he caught his breath. 'This is one mean scene,' he whispered.

Up on the butte The Hunter fed more bullets into his Winchester: .44 calibre slugs punched along by forty grains of black powder, a charge more deadly than any carbine's that could bring down a bear or bison at a mile. He could have killed the stranger's horse, but, no, he was going to have that skewbald. He snapped the magazine shut and levered another bullet into the breech. He had plenty to spare. Two belts of them slung criss-cross fashion over his shoulders. Beneath his hat, with its single feather, his coal-black hair, long and lank, was held back by a scarlet bandanna sweatband. His green eyes glimmered in his swarthy face as he looked out across the folds of hills descending to the tableland and the stark yellow cliffs of the huge canyon. Suddenly he saw a spurt of dust and a horse and rider emerge from a ravine. He steadied the long, blue octagonal barrel back on its rock and squinted along the sights, lining up the pinpoint at the end of the barrel between the buckhorn sight and aimed, unerringly, at the stranger's side, moving the rifle around as he rode. His finger took first squeeze of the trigger, then relaxed. No, why waste a slug? He was just beyond range.

The Hunter raised himself and stood tall, tossing his striped *rebozo* back across his gun arm, and watched the *Americano* go riding away on his spirited horse, on across the tawny flats, on into the shadowed ridges and buttes, slashed with long, deep rims of cliffs. 'He is going nowhere,' he whispered. 'He has no place to go.'

SEVEN

The magnificence of the Grand Canyon could only barely be described in words. One had to stand on the edge of this mile-deep, eighteen-mile-wide gorge and see it with one's own eyes. Particularly at sunset, with the cliffs illuminated in all their glowing colours and velvet shadows, with the Colorado river below looking like a mere silver stream, did it become even more awesome. Sally stood on the viewing point at Papps Peak and breathed it all in, perhaps for the last time.

Percy Papps had had the foresight to see that this natural viewing point on the cliff edge was as good as a goldmine. He had carted in timber and built a shanty to sell 'souvenirs', bits of canyon rock, or other gimcrack mementoes like table mats and 'Grand Canyon' painted chamber pots. He cooked meals for visitors and had palliasses on the floor for them to stay the night, all at sky-high prices. He was stashing the cash away like some boomtown rat.

He hired out mules for there was a steep goat-trail descending to the bed of the turbulent river. Billy Roberts was not devoid of courage and high spirits, when he wasn't imbibing the other kind, and the day before he had embarked on the trip down. But their pack mule had slipped and tumbled five hundred feet to lie prone and, obviously, dead. Sally had foolishly screamed, and beseeched Billy not to go on. So they had returned to the safety of Percy Papps' Peak.

'Aw, there ain' no use hanging around here, Sal,' Billy said, as he sauntered over to join her. 'I know you've got some cash tucked away, hell knows where from, but Papps' prices are crazy. Two dollars for steak and spuds! Holy Jeesis! I'll tell the stage boys to get the horses harnessed and we'll set off home.'

'I guess so, Billy,' she murmured as he put an arm around her waist and tenderly kissed her cheek. 'But you promise we won't stop in Cameron City?'

'Aw, Sal, I'd like a chance to win back some of the dough they took off me. I figure I can do it this time.'

Sally sighed, deeply, for she knew the strength of the terrible urge that possessed him to gamble, like an alcoholic's need for drink. 'Don't be a fool, Billy. We need our money. Cameron City's a corrupt town. It's way out here a law unto itself, owned by one powerful man and his cronies. You don't think even if you won, he'd let someone like you walk away with his cash?'

'He ain't that bad. It's a straight house he runs.'

Sally tried to change the subject, leaning on the

rickety rail of the viewing point and staring out over the canyon. 'Ain't it beautiful, Billy? Can't you be happy, just us two together? Why do you always hanker to go running off to some gaming hell?'

'It's just an idea, Sal.' He kissed her lips, squeezing her to him, her firm, up-tilted bosom in the cotton dress, pressing against his chest. 'Come on, lend me just a hundred bucks outa that poke you got tucked away. I'll double it for us.'

'Ha!' She laughed, turning away. 'You hope!'

'Life's short, Sal. We're only young once. We gotta take risks, enjoy ourselves. Just think of the millions of years this damn canyon's been here. They figure the first white man to see it was Coronado on his march north in 1540. That's more than three centuries ago. When you think of things like that what consequence is a li'l flutter on the tables?'

'You're not getting round me,' she smiled. 'Coronado, indeed!'

'He thought this gorge couldn't be crossed, but John Wesley Powell proved otherwise only fifteen years ago. For three months he braved the tumultous rapids of that river down there, the last unknown river in the good ole USA.'

'So, Mr Papps has been telling you all this. He ought to when he charges five dollars for a hard bed on the floor. And I've had to pay the stage driver ten dollars to stay put for another day. It's daylight robbery. He's being paid to give the horses a nice rest.'

'It's business, Sal. What I'm saying is that it goes to prove a man can do anything if he tries. Come on, Sal, it's only a hundred I need.'

'A hundred! We could buy a damn house for that and a bit of land. No, Billy, it's my money and I'm putting it to good use.'

'We'll see.' He surlily, and abruptly, pushed her loving hands aside, and walked back to the stage coach inside which the wiry driver, Josh Wiggins, and his shotgun, the well-fed Tubby Hayes, were taking their ease. 'OK, boys. We're moving out. I wanna be back in Cameron City tonight.'

Every time he looked around, as fast as he urged his big skewbald, The Hunter was there, a mile or two away. It was as if he were a *vaquero* rounding up a wild horse, going this way and the other, blocking his every means of escape. His mustang might not have speed, but it had stamina, and, like a Mexican *vaquero*, he rode easy in the saddle, his body hardened, muscled, subconsciously aware of every twist, turn, or stumble the beast between his legs might make. Sometimes it seemed like he was an automaton, an insentient being pursuing him that could never be shaken off. Although he was 'only a half-breed' as men might disparagingly remark, he had all the cunning, shrewdness, contempt for privation and danger, and the ability to read sign that distinguishes the full-blooded aboriginal. No, Luke knew that The Hunter was not a man to underestimate.

Luke had been riding all night, and, except for the brief break for coffee at dawn, dramatically disturbed, on and on through the morning as the sun blazed down its full heat nearing the meridian. The skewbald had a big heart, but how much longer could he go on? Soon he would have to make a stand. And it looked like it might be right now, for he had come to the edge, once again, of the Great Divide.

'Hail, what's happened here?' he whispered, through parched lips. 'The Great Sculptor sure didn't carve this out in six days.'

He climbed, stiffly, from his horse and stood on the edge of the yawning gulf, looking a mile down at the mighty river which from this height appeared to be little more than a trickling stream.

'*Hola!*' A voice from the rocks to one side of him made him spin around, his hand going to the butt of his Remington and he had it out, thumbing the hammer back.

'Chay, *amigo*.' The middle-aged Indian squatted on a rock raised his right hand to show he was unarmed. 'You no wan' gun.'

'Yeah?' The man's black hair was streaked with grey, tied by a rawhide filet, and he wore knee-high moccasins and a rough cloth costume beneath a wide *rebozo* of black and white geometrical design. 'What the hell you doin' here?' Luke asked.

The Indian shrugged and waved his hand airily towards some scrubby yellow sheep that were scattered along the edge of the great chasm. 'Thees my land.'

'Your land? You mean the reservation? What tribe are you?'

'Havasupai. For many years we prisoners of Spanish. Now Great Father in Washington give us thees land.'

Luke glanced around at the bare, bleak plateau country where it seemed that neither man nor beast could survive for long and drawled, 'That was mighty generous of him. How the hell I get down into that canyon?'

'Jump?' The Indian's solemn features split into a grin. 'Fast way down.'

'Huh! Another joker, thass all I need.' The Texan took a swig of the lukewarm water in his wooden canteen, and poured some in his palm for the horse to nuzzle at. 'Ain't there a pony trail down?'

'*Sí.*' The Havasupai pointed west to another promontory of the canyon. 'Percy's Peak. You watch out for Percy. He cheat you.'

'Yeah, well thass the last thing I'm worried about right now.' There appeared to be smoke from a cabin on the high promontory. Only about five miles away, but that was as the crow flies. 'I ain't a bird. How the hell do I git there?'

'You go back to trail.' The Indian pointed back along the edge of a deep gulf that cut them off from the promontory. 'It easy. Follow sheep path.'

'It might be easy if some bastard wasn't trying to kill me.' The Texan replaced the cork stopper in the canteen. He was getting low on water, too, and with some desperation, pointed eastwards.

'What's along there?'

'Marble Canyon. But you cut off by Little Colorado canyon. If you wan' go there you got to go back way you come and cross river.'

'Yeah, easier said than done. Looks like he's got me corralled, don't it?'

'Who?'

Luke didn't have time to reply. For answer there came the ominous shriek of a rifling bullet and the clap of a rifle fired from the distance, and, as it spurted dust near his boots, he leaped back into the saddle and set the skewbald cantering away down the edge of the cliffside, heading west, keeping his head low. The Havasupai watched him go and shrugged. These *Americanos*, always behaving strangely. But discretion bade him pick up his basket and start moving his flock quickly eastwards.

'Jeez!' Luke let out his breath with relief as he reached the cover of an overhang, but he knew it was only temporary safety. Sooner or later he would have to come up against his adversary. A man with a carbine versus a man with a rifle. Verdict: no contest. 'Where's this damn sheep path gone to?' He scoured the ground for its faint trace. 'We gotta git outa here. We gotta reach that trail 'fore he does, hoss.'

Brad Cameron had set a marksman with a rifle to keep a watch out from the top of a column of rock a few miles out on the trail for any strangers, who were few and far between, riding into town. Ethan McShay was bored with the assignment, but he had found a bit of shade under a ledge of rock and had a bottle for company. Suddenly, late on the second day of his watch, he saw a bearded man, in a suit with a low-crowned hat, riding towards him. 'Hold it right there, mister,' he hollered. 'What you doing in these parts?'

The stranger peered up and saw the glint of sun on the rifle. 'I've got business to transact with a Mr Cameron.'

'Yeah, he's been expectin' you.' Ethan levered his rifle. 'And you ain't welcome.'

The man tried to snatch his own carbine from the saddle boot and simultaneously wheel his horse around, jerking at the reins. But, too late! Ethan's bullet smashed through his spine and he fell, dragged away by one boot in his bentwood stirrup.

The shootist ran back to his own bronco and spurred it down the slope to catch up with the loose horse. He released the dead stranger and pulled a wallet from his pocket. 'I thought as much.' He grinned as he read a card: 'Federal Bureau of Investigation.'

'You won't be doin' no investigatin' here, *hombre.*'

Ethan stuffed the man's watch and wallet in his own pocket and dragged him to the edge of the trail where there happened to be a convenient cliff. He sent the corpse tumbling down into a rocky *arroyo.*

'You're gonna make the vultures a nice breakfast.' He apprised the nark's horse. 'Not a bad bit of hossmeat. You should make me twenty dollars.' He rode back to town leading the stranger's mustang alongside him. 'Cameron's gonna be pleased,' he said.

EIGHT

Luke Hackman's heart lifted when he finally spotted the winding dust trail that led from Cameron City, forty miles away, to Papps' Peak. But it fell again as there was the crack of rifle fire up ahead of him, cutting him off from possible freedom. 'Goddam!' Instinct made him haul his horse around as, almost simultaneously, a lead slug ploughed into the dust. Another whistled past his head as he sent the skew-bald haring towards a pile of rocks that reared beside the trail. He dived from the horse, abandoning it to its own devices, and scurried for cover behind the curiously-shaped rock pile, scattered thuswise by indiscriminate nature. He eyed its ledges apprehensively as he began to haul himself upwards, hoping against hope that he didn't put his hand on a sun-basking diamondback. When he reached the crest he peered across towards the chisel-shaped termination of a high red butte from which puffs of powder smoke were drifting. It was time to live or die.

'Come on you hell's spawn,' he hollered out, his

words echoing across the valley. 'Come and get me. Or you can try.'

There was momentary silence and then The Hunter appeared, riding his mustang out of cover, his Winchester balanced butt-down on one knee. He had nothing to fear at that range from Hackman's carbine. With delicate grace his mustang went clipping along the sheer surface of the base of the butte until it met the valley floor of rocks, sagebrush and cactus and it began weaving its way across towards the Texan. The Hunter rode with arrogant self-assurance, unhurried, taking his time. It was as if the rest of the world no longer existed, it was just these two men alone in the wilderness involved in their fight.

It was not that Luke Hackman did not know fear, the pounding of the heart, the trickle of sweat down his temple, even dread, remorse, regret that any moment his life might end. But another emotion stirred within him, a warrior instinct, a hatred of the enemy, an urge to kill or be killed. He was tired of being pushed around.

'Come on,' he growled, as he crouched in the rocks, his Sharps hugged tight into his shoulder. 'Come closer, you bastard.'

He glanced around and saw that his skewbald had wandered away from the trail into the shadow of the rocks, out of The Hunter's vision. Maybe, if he had no horse, he would be less sure of himself. It was a long shot. A good two hundred yards. Hackman squinted down his sights as The Hunter came on. He squeezed the trigger and his bullet tore into the mustang's chest, making it kick and roll over, screaming its death agony as blood pumped from its heart. The Hunter had jumped clear and was taking cover behind his dying horse.

'There, you lousy 'breed,' Luke yelled. 'You weren't expecting that, were you? Thought I'd never git you at that range. Come on, you murdering coward, where's your guts now?'

He wanted to get the 'breed mad, make him lose control. Underestimating a Texan was his first mistake. 'Thought I was just some no-good roller of craps, did you?' he called. 'Thought I was sceered of you? Think again, pal. Come on, what you waitin' for? You want my hoss you gotta git past me.'

The Hunter was swearing volubly in border Spanish, but Luke was no stranger to such language and replied in kind, tauntingly. 'What's the matter, squitface? You down on your knees sayin' a prayer over your dead mustang? He's just a heap of crowbait now.'

The 'breed gave a scream of anger and leaped over the mustang, dodging forward, jumping from cover to cover, stalking the man up in the pile of rocks, his dark face a mask of murderous hatred. Luke let him come and and let him have another shot that put a hole in his tall black hat and made him bob down. 'Yeah, grovel, damn you. Don't like some of your own treatment, do you? You frontier scum never do.'

Again The Hunter gave a howl of rage and raising his rifle splattered the rocks wildly with bullets, levering the Winchester until his magazine was empty. Luke flattened himelf as bullets bounced off the rocks, one almost parting his hair, buzzing around him like hornets on the warpath. He counted every explosion and at the fifteenth, rose to one knee, taking careful aim, returning the leaden compliments, making The Hunter roll to one side. For once The Hunter was being hunted.

But not for long. Luke searched the rocks for sight of him. Either he was taking his time reloading or he was down on his belly crawling like a snake towards him. And there he was! Closer than he had anticipated, just a hundred yards off. Luke sent a slug spinning towards him, but the man knew he had only a single shot and was up on his legs charging towards him, levering the Winchester, and firing as he ran. It was Luke's turn to duck down again.

The Texan grinned to himself as he reloaded, his heart pounding. In some ways he was enjoying this. There was nothing like a taste of action to stimulate a man's senses. Hell! Why not go out in a blaze of glory?

'Hey!' he yelled, after The Hunter had wasted another fifteen shots trying to flush him from the rocks. 'Ye'll never git me in here. But, I'm willing to come out. I'm sick of this. How about we go for the fast draw?'

There was silence as the 'breed considered this. Luke had discovered that the higher the risk for the pot the more likely a man was to throw everything he had into the game. Especially wild gamblers of Indian blood. 'Come on, pal, are you going to ante up or not?'

'Fair enough, stranger,' The Hunter yelled back.

'Fast draw it is. Come on out.'

'Let's see you toss that Winchester away first.'

'OK,' The Hunter snarled, standing and throwing the rifle away into the scrub. 'Maybe I'll have better luck with Sam Colt.'

'Maybe.' Luke rose to his feet, too, his Sharps still in his grip and for moments he was tempted to let the hired killer have it in the guts. But, bad as The Hunter was, he couldn't shoot him down in cold blood. He threw the Sharps to the foot of the rocks and ploughed down on his boot-heels through the scree. Now they were standing sixty paces apart eyeing each other like two poker players across the table. 'Come on, let's deal.'

The Hunter flicked his poncho back across one shoulder and his long fingers snaked towards his gun-butt holstered low on his thigh, delicately checking it with his fingertips. 'I've got the trump,' he yelled, as he started striding towards the Texan.

'Whadda ya mean?'

'A bullet through your head.' At that the 'breed slid the .45 from his holster, and began fanning the hammer with his horny left palm. 'Die, *gringo*.'

Luke jerked his Remington free. The 'breed had started shooting before he expected him to. Luke wasn't an expert shootist and needed to get in close range for this duel. Somehow it was like a dream, or nightmare, what must have been a few seconds of ear-shattering explosions extended into a timeless dance of death.

The Hunter's first slug nicked his ear-lobe, his second ripped his sleeve, his third whistling harmlessly past as Luke stepped aside. He aimed at his opponent's belt buckle relying on the kick of the big Remington to give him a heart shot. But it was too high and creased the 'breed's cheek. He strode forward to get in closer. He gritted his teeth, held his arm outstretched, and squeezed the trigger. Got him! The part-Indian gave a grimace of pain and clutched at his shoulder but at the same time Luke saw another plume of smoke and felt like he'd been hit in the thigh with a sledgehammer. He tumbled back into the dust on his side of the trail. On the other side The Hunter raised his Colt, concentrating to finish him. . . .

There was a rush of wheels on the gravel and a whinny of horses as Josh Wiggins hauled then in with a shouted 'Whoa-agh thar!' His guard, Tubby Hayes, leaned out, pointing his shotgun at The Hunter as the stagecoach came to a halt between the two men. 'What in tarnation's goin' on here, mister? You put that gun down, pronto, you hear?'

The Hunter swayed on his feet as flies honed in on the blood seeping from his shoulder. 'Get out my friggin' way.' He raised the Colt and fired pointblank into Tubby's surprised face. The bullet took half his jaw away and exited through his skull in a mess of blood and brains. What remained of Tubby slowly tumbled into the dust.

'Hail!' Josh froze with the reins in his hands. 'This ain't nuthin' to do with me, mister.'

'Move that coach along, you hear. Not too far. Just a few paces. I'll be riding with you back to Cameron City.'

88

'Sure, mister.' Wiggins did as he was bid, and as the coach rattled forwards, Hackman was revealed lying on the far side of the trail, clutching at his knee, his face agonized.

Luke was in a haze of shock for the impact of the bullet was equivalent to a four-tonne weight dropping on his leg from a great height. It had crashed through flesh, nerves and muscle. But, in spite of the intense pain he was still conscious of immense danger so he struggled to raise the Remington, thumb the hammer and send a shot flying at The Hunter, grinning at him from across the way. His bullet went wild and the 'breed was levelling his Colt, the deathly hole aimed at his heart to finish him. It looked like this was the end. 'You win, pal,' Luke muttered.

But suddenly The Hunter spun in his tracks as a slug whistled past his jaw. He turned to see Billy had stepped from the coach and was blamming away at him with a cheap 'storekeeper'. The slug meant for Luke he put, instead, unerringly into Billy's chest and the youth slumped against the stage with a groan of despair.

The gunman turned back to Luke who, past caring, had laid aside his Remington to nurse his shattered thigh, staring at his blood pouring out, surprised at how red and how much of it there was. 'So long, sucker,' the 'breed snarled. 'You lose.' But when he pulled the trigger there was only an empty click. He had spent all his lead. He gave a last snarl of anger, hurled the revolver at Luke, before he fell back, collapsing, unconscious, in the dust.

Sally was down on her knees screaming her shock, patting at her husband's face. 'Billy, don't . . . no . . . don't leave me.'

'It ain' no use, missy,' Josh drawled. 'He's day-ed. Same as poor ole Tubby who nevuh done no one no dang harm.'

'Why?' the girl sobbed. 'Oh, Billy, why did you do it, you fool? Why get in the way? I told you not to.'

'He died brave, missy. C'mon, less see how this other guy is. That feller would have kilt him for sure iffen we hadn't happened along.'

'Oh, God forbid that we did,' she cried. 'Why? Why us?'

'You jest happened to be in the wrong place at the wrong time, thassall.' Josh knelt beside Luke. 'How ya feelin', mister? Losin' a bit of blood thar. Here, I'll put your belt round yer thigh as a turrnay-key. We gotta git ya into the coach. Can ya hobble up on one leg. Here, hold on to me. Thar ya. We gotta git ya to the quack.'

By dint of determination and an effort to ignore the pain that was making his head swim Luke managed to get seated inside the coach. 'We can't leave Billy here,' Sally Roberts screamed and she and the driver hauled him inside, too, to prop beside Luke.

'Come on, less git Tubby in. Thar's room for him beside you, gal. He kin ride in style for his last spin 'stead of up on the box.'

After they had struggled to put both the wounded and the dead inside, the girl asked, 'What about that other one?'

'Aw, thar ain' no room for him. 'Sides, he looks like he's through, or soon will be by the time the coyotes're finished with him.'

'Well, he killed Billy, so it serves him right,' Sally agreed as she climbed back in the coach.

'Hang on, folks, it's gonna be a bumpy ride,' Josh yelled, as he slammed shut the door.

'Hey, what about my hoss?' Luke called, weakly. 'Cain't leave him behind.'

But Josh was already cracking his whip across the ears of his team, sending them into a wild lope along the trail. 'Yaugh-hay! Git up, thar, ye lop-eared mokes. Cameron City here we come.'

Sally Roberts stared at the Texan who sprawled beside her dead husband, his shattered leg outstretched. Every bump of the stagecoach as it went rattling along made him grimace in agony. Beneath his tan his face was becoming pallid. He was losing too much blood. She raised her skirt and ripped away her white, lace-trimmed petticoat. She knelt between his legs, took the knife from his scabbard, and cut the fringed *chaparejos*, cutting his trousers, too, away from the wound. A nasty bloody hole. She made a pad of part of the material and used the rest to tie a tight bandage. She jerked the buckle of the belt tourniquet tighter making him wince.

'What you doing?' he asked, opening his eyes.

'Trying to help you.'

'You look kinda nice down there between my knees, it suits you.' He forced a grin and reached out

91

to caress her hair and nape. 'You're a good kid.'

She drew away from him and looked out of the window. 'We've an awful long way to go.'

'We should make it by nightfall. But I ain't so sure there's any point in me going to Cameron City. They're trying to kill me. You got any of that cash left?'

'Yes, a good bit of it.'

'There's a Mex farm on the outskirts as we roll in. Maybe, if you give 'em some dough, they might let me hide out there for a coupla days. I hear they're none too fond of Brad Cameron, either. He killed their kin.'

'Yes, I'll do that, I'll tell the driver to haul in there. And I'll spend money on getting the doctor to visit you. Can I use some of it to bury Billy?'

'Yeah, it's yourn. I'm just borrowing some back. You keep what's left and get outa that town fast. It ain't a good place to be.' He closed his eyes and seemed to lapse into sleep, but opened them again. 'Sal, don't go causing a stink about this, demanding justice, 'cause there ain't none in that town. The sheriff's on Cameron's payroll. You start causing trouble all you'll get is a bullet in your back.'

'What about you? How will you get away?'

'I still got my Sharps and my Remington, haven't I? I'll be OK. This will soon heal. At least, I hope so.'

'You'll be needing some money.' She fumbled in her purse. 'Here, take half of this.'

He tried to wave her away but she stuffed the dollar bills into his shirt pocket. 'I'll pay you back,' he muttered.

'Don't be ridiculous.'

'What a fine party this is.' He tried to force another grin as he looked at the two corpses, their faces discoloured by death, rigor mortis setting in. 'Don't forget, bury Billy, then go. Forget all this.'

She opened her palms, pleadingly, her blue eyes wide. 'Forget? How can I forget? I want revenge.'

NINE

Ants had already made a start investigating The Hunter, and turkey vultures had descended to hop and croak nearby, making dashes at him to pluck at his clothes, unsure whether he was dead or alive. Soon coyotes would gather at the feast. The two Indians who found him shook their heads and hauled him on to what they presumed to be his horse, the skewbald. They took them up the trail to Percy Papps' cabin on the promontory.

Percy gave the Indians a bottle of raw whiskey and they cleared off, happy enough. They did not want to be accused of robbing the 'breed. Percy had no such scruples, quickly going through the man's pockets and extracting fifty bucks from his wallet. As he did so The Hunter stirred and opened his eyes, so Percy quickly tucked the wallet into his own pocket.

'What the hell happened to me?' The Hunter instinctively clutched at his shoulder wound and groaned. 'Oh, yeah, I remember now.'

'What did happen, mister?' Papps was sorry the man had come round. He had been planning to dump his body in the canyon and keep his horse. 'Don't move. You got a hole in your shoulder. I was jest gonna clean it up.'

'Yeah?' The Hunter eyed him, suspiciously. 'How did I get here?'

'Two of them Havasupai found ya. They hauled you in on your bronc.'

'My bronc?'

'Yeah, the patch. Nice horse.'

'Oh, yeah.' He watched Papps fetch a basin of water and start cleaning the bullet hole. 'What happened to the other one?'

'Who?'

'The guy who bushwhacked me?'

'Hell knows. You were all they found.'

'That lousy Texan backshooter musta got away.' He lay back on one of Papps' palliases and studied the bloody hole. It wasn't a bad wound by his standards, but painful enough. 'I gotta git after him.'

'You ain't going nowhere just yet, mister. You gotta rest. But you're one lucky sonuvagun. The bullet seems to have gawn right through the side of your upper chest. A clear hole through the soft flesh and out the back. It ain't lodged no place.'

'Yeah.' The Hunter gasped as Papps probed at him. 'Hey, take it easy, that hurts.'

'I'll bandage you up.' As he was plugging the hole and winding cloth around The Hunter's broad, muscled chest, Papps muttered, 'Made a mess of your shirt. I can sell you a new one, if you want?'

He wished he hadn't mentioned money for as soon as he did The Hunter reached with his good arm for his discarded shirt and felt the pocket.

'Somebody's stole my wallet.'

'Musta been that bushwhacker. Or them thievin' Indians.'

'Yeah, an' maybe it was you.' The Hunter slipped out his Colt revolver and put it to Papps throat. 'Empty your own damn pockets.'

Papps trembled and stuttered as he pretended he had nothing of value on him. 'I ain't got nothing, mister, I swear to God.'

'Empty that right hand coat pocket. Easy now. Don't try nuthin'. Come on, let's see the lining.'

Percy Papps produced the wallet with an air of surprise. 'Oh, this? Is this yours? They said they picked it up along the trail. I was going to hand it in. I swear by my mother's grave.'

'You kin go an' jine her, you scumbag.' Anger flashed through The Hunter and the Colt roared in his fist, the bullet going up through the chin into Papps' brain, killing him. The Hunter got to his feet, standing unsteadily, as gunsmoke wafted. 'Nobody robs me.'

He stepped over Papps's body, flicking ants from his hair. He took a white shirt from a pile and pulled it on awkwardly over his wounded left shoulder, his arm stiff and throbbing. He found a bottle of corn whiskey and took a slug. For the rest of the night he dozed, fitfully. In the morning he searched for the miser's money. 'He must have it somewhere,' he muttered, and finally found a crock of gold pieces and greenbacks hidden in a hole behind the cabin. He fried himself a slice of bacon, sipped coffee, unhurriedly. He fed and watered the skewbald, saddled up and, with some difficulty, because of his shoulder, hauled himself on board. He felt a bit woozy from loss of blood but he would be OK. He cantered the skewbald back to where the fight had been, found his Winchester in the sagebrush, and put the horse to a fast lope back along the trail to Cameron City.

The Hunter gritted out as he rode, 'I got a score to settle with that Texan dude.'

'We'll find him,' Brad Cameron said. 'He can't have got far. I need his damn body if my plan's gonna work. I want all you boys to scour the neigh-bourhood. Try all the farms. Somebody's hiding him someplace. We shoulda quizzed that stage driver. He musta known where Hackman jumped off.'

'He's gone, boss.' Nelson Eades was leaned against the bar in the saloon amid ten other of Cameron's hired thugs. 'He'll be in Flagstaff by now.'

'How about the gal? She was there. She must know something.'

'She's buryin' her husband today.'

'Well, as soon as he's planted grab her. Take her to the cabin. We'll soon persuade her to talk.'

Nelson grinned, lecherously. 'I'll personally take care of persuadin' her, Mr Cameron.'

'Don't louse up, Nelson. Do what you like to her but make her talk. We need to know all she knows. And we might need to use her as a hostage. So keep her a prisoner. Don't kill her. At least, not yet awhile. Although, she probably knows too much than is healthy for her.'

Nelson grinned at the other bully boys. 'It'll be a pleasure, boss. Jimmy, you come with me. The rest of you make a tour of the outlying *ranchos*.'

'Yes,' Cameron shouted. 'And make sure you tear apart those Mex rat-holes. He's hidden someplace. A hundred dollars to the man who brings his body in.'

'We don't wan' your money,' Isabella Chavez had said, when Sally had offered her ten dollars to let the Texan hide out at her farm. Ten dollars was a lot of cash to a *peon*. 'Do not insult us. Anybody who enemy of Cameron is our friend.'

'It ain' no use me stayin' in the *casa*,' Luke said, as Josh Wiggins half-carried him from the stagecoach. 'They'll come lookin'. Ain't there no place they won't look?'

The haughty Isabella, with her long black hair, in the black dress of mourning, studied the fugitive with her dark, dolorous eyes. 'First we must clean that wound,' she murmured. 'Bring him in the house and lay him down.'

'The slug's still in there.' Luke gave a gasp of pain. 'Can you dig it out, pal, 'fore you go?'

'I can try.' Wiggins looked doubtful, but pulled his Bowie and went to sterilize it in the flame of their oven fire. 'This is a bad business. What am I gonna tell the sheriff when I bring those bodies in?'

'Tell him The Hunter held up the stage but you shot him down with your sidearm after Billy and your guard got killed. You left him lyin' there. No need to say nuthin' about me. Just hightail it outa town.'

'Waal, OK.' Josh had accepted the ten dollars from Sally. He didn't have Mexican pride about such matters. To a Yankee a buck was a buck. 'I'm riskin' my job coverin' up evee-dence an' gittin' mixed up in this. Maybe even my life from the sound of thangs.'

'C'mon. Git on with it. Give him another ten, Sally, to keep him quiet.' Luke didn't say much after that, just bit on a bullet as the driver probed the sharp point into his flesh. 'It's lodged 'ginst the bone. Don't see no broken bits. Thar! Got ya, ya varmint.' Josh fished out the bloody slug. 'I'll keep this as a souvenir. Gimme the powder outa one of his bullets.'

'What for?' Sally had asked.

'You'll see, missy. No, give it me.' He used the knife to extract the lead, and tipped the powder from the casing on to the wound. He struck a match and lit it. 'Thar. Thass what they call cauterizin' the wound.'

'Aagh!' Luke could not help crying out at the fiery pain, but he gasped with relief that it was done. Now he had a fifty-fifty chance the bullet hole would heal. 'What the hell's that?'

The old woman, Rosa, had prepared a poultice of herbs, leaves and a pungent ointment and was kneeling down applying it, tying bandages. '*Buena*,' she cooed. '*Buena.*'

'It is my grandmother's medicine, handed down by her mother,' Isabella had assured him. 'It is good.'

'Waal, if I lose my leg I'm blamin' you three. Anyway, Sal, no need to send for the doc now. They would probably follow him. He cain't do no more.'

'Think yourself lucky, mister. Six inches higher an' that'd have bin your marital prospects gone.'

'Yeah, well, where the hell you gonna hide me?'

'I can only theenk the well. Don' worry, it is dry now.'

They had half-carried him, hobbling out towards their allotment, which now, without water, was withered and parched. The animals, too, the *burros*, the cow, the pigs, the dogs, rib-thin and listless, stood dying on their feet from thirst. What was left of the family had barely enough water for their own needs and that was disappearing fast. Behind some rocks was a ten-feet-wide well that had dried up. Isabella had removed its rotted boards and they had put a rope around the Texan's shoulders and lowered him twenty feet down. 'Don't worry, *hombre*,' Josh had called. 'You only got spiders and snakes to worry about now.'

Luke groaned as he lay down on the stones and rested his leg. 'Toss me my Sharps down, old timer. I might be needing it.' He had caught the carbine and laid it beside him. 'Sally, you do your buryin' and git outa that town, you hear? It ain't safe. Go home.'

The girl had peered over the edge and called, 'What will you do, Luke?'

'I'll be fine. I'll rest up this leg then I got some questions I want answering. Pull them planks across. It'll give me some shade. So long, and thanks, y'all.'

They had pulled the planks back across and Isabella had tossed some hay over them. She had wiped a trickle of sweat from her forehead, and her hair from her eyes, which were defiant, if worried. 'He will be fine. I would rather die than betray him.' She crossed herself. 'I pray to God the gringo will bring us vengeance.'

'My husband died defending me from an evil armed robber,' Sally told the undertaker. 'I want a solid oak coffin with brass handles.'

'Oak's expensive,' the undertaker sniffed. 'Any damn wood is in these parts. Most fellas git wrapped in sacking. At best a pine box.'

'He was a good man,' she replied. 'He loved me. I want him to have the best.'

And an impressive funeral it was: two proud dappled grey horses, ostrich feathers tossing on their heads, pulling the ornate hearse in which Billy rested, the undertaker like a lanky crow in his black frock coat and crepe-swathed top hat, a priest, his umbrella raised for shade, sitting side-saddle on his *burro* and Sally, in a black silk dress and veil, following on foot.

She was the only mourner. Other folk paused to watch as she passed, men removing their hats, their faces grim. They had seen too many buryings in this town. Wise not to get involved. A gang of men, idling outside the saloon in the shade of the canopy, shrugged and grinned at death, their eyes cold. They had seen too much death for it to worry them. Nelson Eades leaned back against the wall, one knee raised, and licked his thin lips. 'She sure is a purty li'l thang, ain't she?' he purred. 'Can you jest imagine her nice white body when I rip apart that black silk. C'mon, Jimmy, less go watch.'

The priest had muttered words in Latin incomprehensible to her and they had lowered Billy's coffin into the hole in the dirt. The priest had sprinkled holy water and the undertaker and his men had shovelled back the dirt and trooped off. They climbed on to the hearse and returned to the town. Was that all there was at the end of a man's life? Sally knelt in the deserted graveyard. At least she had got him a decent headstone. 'William Roberts, 1868–1888. Shot by an assassin. May vengeance be the Lord's.'

'You allus was a durn fool, Billy,' she murmured, 'but I loved you.'

Suddenly, she heard the crunch of gravel under boots, and two shadows appeared of men standing over her. There was a caustic laugh as one of them drawled, 'He's gawn to the Big Gambler in the sky. There ain' no use you prayin' over him. You gonna come along with us. Don't you give us no trouble and we won't hurt you, gal.'

Sally looked up at Nelson Eades grinning down at her, and another man with hard looks beneath the shadow brim of his hat. They were in range clothes and slung with iron. She tried to dart away, but in vain. They caught hold of her and marched her to the graveyard gates.

'Git up on that spare hoss.' Eades backhanded her across the cheek. 'Hurry up, you bitch. Or you want us to drag you by your heels?'

TEN

Isabella was woken early in the morning by the clatter of horses' hoofs, the rattle of bridles, the sound of gringos shouting roughly to each other. In a panic she gathered her three children, who slept in her bed, around her as a revolver butt was hammered on the wooden door. 'Open up,' a man shouted.

'Better open it than have them break it down,' she said to Rosa who slid back the wooden latch, and stepped aside as three men burst in led by The Hunter.

'Where is he?' the 'breed snarled, raising his rifle and pointing it at Isabella and the cowering children.

'Who?' The young woman was still in her white night shift. 'What do you want here, murderer?'

'Don't play games with me.' The 'breed viciously smashed the rifle butt into a big *olla* of water that had been in the family for generations, and began destroying what other few household possessions he could see. 'You know who. The *Americano*. The Texan. Where you hiding him?'

'I don't know what you are talking about,' Isabella screamed at him. 'I know of no Texan. Why don't you leave us alone? You have killed my father, my mother, my two brothers, what more do you want?'

For answer the half-breed snatched hold of her eldest son's hair and dragged him from her putting a knife to eight-year-old Ernesto's throat. 'Speak or I slit him. You scum breed like rats. You think anyone will miss him? Where is he?'

'*Señor*, please, spare my son. If I knew I would tell you. But I don't know. I cannot help you.'

There was a screaming and wailing as her two widowed sisters-in-law were dragged from their adjoining *casas* with their children and were given the same interrogation.

'For Chris'sakes tell 'em to stop that din.' The Hunter tossed the boy aside, and stormed outside, laying about him with his rifle, using it as a cudgel. 'Where's the Texan?' The Hunter roared. 'There's twenty dollars to the one who leads me to him.'

Isabella dared hardly breathe as she watched her sisters-in-laws' eyes widen. Twenty dollars! What was the Texan to them? Did they really believe this widow-maker would give it to them once he had found him? Could they give the American away?

No. The women glanced at her and shook their heads, dumbly, pulling their children into them. Old Rosa was pointing her finger at the men who had been searching the houses, barns and fields. 'I curse you, you fiends. You have taken our water, killed our men, murdered my fine daughter. I curse you to your graves. . . .'

The Hunter had had enough. The screaming and sobbing was getting on his nerves. He was tempted to wipe out the whole brood with a volley from his Winchester, in fact his finger itched to, but Cameron had said to cool down, that there had been enough killing. The only one he wanted dead was the Texan.

'Come on,' he shouted, leaping on to his new skewbald. 'Let's go. But' – he pointed a finger, warning – 'if you are hiding him we will burn you all down.'

Luke Hackman slipped in and out of a fever, sweat pouring from him, drifting in and out of strange dreams. At one point he heard screams, at another children singing. Sometimes daylight filtered through the boards and their camouflage of hay but he had little idea how many days had passed. The pain throbbed in his leg. His main fear was that gangrene would set in, that it would have to be sawn off by the doc. But, one morning, when he inspected it, there was no gangrenous stench. The bleeding had dried up. He used his carbine as a crutch and managed to get on to his feet. 'Allelujah!' he cried.

The cry of joy was a bad mistake. One of Cameron's men, called One-eyed Jack, had returned to keep an eye on the place. He heard the shout, which seemed to come from a pile of hay. As ugly in nature as he was in looks, he cocked his piece, scraped the hay aside with his boot and saw the rough planks across the well. He kicked one aside, half-leaned over and emptied his revolver wildly down into the well at what he thought was a man lying down there. The blue smoke curled and he peeped over to get a better view. A slug from the Sharps hit him between the eyes as Luke stepped from the cover of the well-side and fired up at him. The *bandido* hit the ground hard beside him, stone dead. Luke gave a whistle of surprise and went over to look at the blanket he had spread over a fallen log to sit on. It was riddled with six holes.

'Bad luck, ole son,' he said, 'you missed me.'

The heads of women and children appeared, staring down at him. 'I wanna get outa here,' he shouted. 'Toss a rope down.'

'What are you going to do?' Isabella chided, after they had managed to haul him to the top. 'You are not well enough to ride.'

'I ain't gonna ride. You're gonna take me into town in the wagon. Least, I hope you are, but I can't guarantee your safety.'

'I will come with you. But what is your plan?'

'I'm gonna try and kill 'em, before they kill me.'

He tried a few tentative steps walking with the aid of the Sharps, but it was agony and he wasn't sure how long the leg would hold out. He saw a big iron plough share and asked, 'Could you wimmin lift that into the wagon? Sorry I ain't much help. Place it on the right-hand side. Yeah, that'll do. Right, you ready to go?'

Isabella insisted she gave him food and drink first, and applied another poultice to the leg wound, as the Texan checked his carbine and revolver. Then as the sun westered they left the farmstead, Isabella driving the mule and wagon slowly but determinedly along the trail. 'I'm entering the town now,' she called back to Luke.

'Right, draw up by Cameron's bank opposite the saloon. I want the sun behind my back. Soon as we're there get down and make a beeline for cover. All hell's gonna break out.'

The Texan was lying in the wagon using the ploughshare as a shield, his carbine poked through the crack in the two boards that was the wagon's side. He peered through the crack at the few bystanders on the sidewalk who watched Isabella pass with curiosity. It was nearly six of the evening when most of the riff-raff gathered in the saloon and when the sun's rays, as it sank over the canyon, would be at their most fiery and dazzling. 'Right, you bastards,' he muttered, 'it's time to roll the dice.'

He knew he had little chance of coming out of this alive, the odds against it were high, but, at least, he might get a few of them before he died, maybe even Cameron himself.

'Cameron,' he yelled at the top of his lungpower, as Isabella halted the wagon and climbed down. 'Here I am. Come and get me.' There was an uncanny silence as the Mexican woman hurried away, then one of Cameron's bully boys edged out of the batwing doors of the Golden Eagle, tugging his revolver from his belt. He was quickly followed by two more men who took up position on the sidewalk, their weapons at the ready.

'Show yourself,' one shouted.

Luke shot him in the throat, and he tumbled down the steps. His second bullet took out another as he tried to back into the saloon. The third man ducked down as the saloon windows were smashed and he and his *compadres* sent a fusillade of shots smashing into the wagon. The bullets spanged off the ploughshare ricocheting away.

Luke gritted his teeth, flinching, expecting the worst, but the iron share protected him. He took another bullet from his belt and fitted it into the Sharps, aiming it at a thug carelessly exposed at a window. Bullseye! He was left spreadeagled over the ledge. 'Got him! Three down.'

As he spoke a slug smashed into the wagon floor behind him. He rolled on to his back and looked up to see Cameron standing on the balcony of the bank, a smoking revolver in his fist. Beside him was the little bald cashier, Cy Cooper, staring down at him, fumbling with the safety catch of a Colt Frontiersman. Luke pulled out his Remington and squeezed the trigger. Cameron jumped back as the bullet grazed his temple, pulling Cy in front of him as a shield. The little man struggled, but Luke's next slug slammed into his abdomen. Cameron held him upright for protection, and tossed him aside as he backed into the bank office.

'Hell take him,' Luke muttered, subjected to such a withering hail of fire from the saloon it was difficult to get a shot in.

Inside the Golden Eagle, however, The Hunter

shouted, 'Hold your fire, men. He's got some kinda protection. We gotta git at him from t'other side.'

The 'breed peered from the side of the broken window. 'Ethan, git up on the roof of the Meat Mart and git a bead on him. Josh, work your way round beside the bank. Harry, make a dash over to the gunshop. When I give the signal we'll rush him. I'll go round to the emporium. Come on, we'll go out the back door.'

'Right,' the man called Ethan shouted. 'You boys give us cover when we charge. Keep him occupied. He's got no chance.'

Over at the bank Brad Cameron was frantically stuffing all the spare cash from his safe into a portmanteau. He couldn't wait to see Hackman killed. It was time to get out. He had two fast horses and a lightweight buggy waiting for him along at the livery for just such an emergency.

'Brad,' Cy Cooper croaked out as he climbed through the window door from the balcony, clutching his side. 'You gotta take me with you. You owe me. We been partners a long time.'

'Too long,' Cameron snarled, putting a bullet from his revolver through his heart. He stepped over the forger. 'Sorry, Cy. I ain't got room for a passenger.'

He clattered down the stairs and slipped out of the back door, listening alertly to the gunbattle, and hurried away along the back of the houses to the stables.

The sky was blood-red, rearing over the town, as

the sun sank in the west, making it nigh impossible for the four gunmen left in the saloon to get a good shot at the man in the wagon across the dirt street.

Alphonse, in his top hat and bow tie, was standing behind the bar in the Golden Eagle while Ruby had not moved from her usual stool as neutral onlookers, who had been enjoying their six o'clock tipple, cowered behind tables.

'If their plan works that cowboy is one dead duck,' Alphonse said to Ruby. 'What a bally shame. I liked that chappie.'

'Yes.' Ruby glanced anxiously at him and downed her whiskey sour. 'I'm sick of this. The odds ain't right. I'm gonna help him.' She took a three-inch derringer from her bag. 'How about you?'

'I'm with you, darlin'.' He opened his carpetbag and brought out a German Luger. 'Charles, my dear boy,' he cooed at the cook, who was kneeling at the window aiming a carbine at the wagon. 'May I have your attention?'

Charley spun around on one knee. 'Yeah, whadda ya want?'

'Your cuisine, my dear fellow is atrocious.' Alphonse smiled sweetly and pointed the Luger at him. 'You deserve to be decimated.'

Charley jerked like a puppet and crumpled into a foetal position, as the three men blamming away from the windows turned to stare at Alphonse with surprise.

'Hey, molly boy,' one roared, 'whose side you on?'

'Guess.' Alphonse and Ruby sents bullets flying as

111

the three men scrambled to fire at them. Too late. They were scattered like ninepins. ' "What fools ye mortals may be." I think that's one to you and three to me, dear girl.'

Meanwhile The Hunter had made his way around to the emporium and looked around to see whether Ethan, Harry and Josh were in place ready to strike. Suddenly a woman in black stepped out on to the sidewalk silhouetted against the blazing sun. The 'breed blinked as he tried to make out who it was and raised his revolver to fire.

'Vengeance!' Isabella tossed back her *rebozo* and swung her father's shotgun his way, spraying death with the first barrel.

The Hunter was propelled six steps back to sprawl in the dust. '*Puta*!' he snarled, trying to raise the Colt once more as blood trickled from the scatter gun pellet-holes in his chest. The second barrel spurted flame and he fell back.

'Die, you fiend,' Isabella whispered. 'That was for my father, my mother, and my two brothers. May their souls rejoice while yours rots in hell.'

She crossed herself, but, glancing up at the Meat Mart she saw Ethan kneeling behind the false front lining the sights of his carbine on the *Americano*'s back. She calmly took Ronaldo's slim hunting rifle from her blanket bundle and sent Ethan catapulting from the rooftop to lie still in the dust. Isabella crossed herself once more.

The sheriff, Hank Finnegan, had been roused from his *siesta* by the shooting and had watched the battle from the sidelines, drawing his sixgun in readiness as he saw Josh by the bank and Harry by the gunshop signal to each other to charge the rear of the wagon, as Luke raised himself on one elbow to try to see what was going on. The fat Finnegan ran after them and edged his way along past the terrified mule to crouch by the wagon side, nodding to the other two to go for it.

Before they could do so, however, Alphonse rolled beneath the mule's belly and came up, smiling, 'Hello!' The startled Finnegan turned to fire but Alphonse's bullet got him through the belly. Simultaneously, Ruby had arrived on the other side. 'Hey, what about me?' she called and, as Harry spun on her, she let him have it with her derringer. He threw up his hands and rolled to one side making Josh's aim go awry.

Alphonse raised his Luger and thudded slugs into Josh's back. The sheriff raised his eyes to him and groaned, 'I thought you was a cream puff.'

'Don't judge by appearances,' Alphonse replied, putting further slugs into them all to finish them.

As the acrid gunsmoke whirled, Luke hauled himself up the side of the wagon and drawled, 'What's happening?'

'A bitter business,' Alphonse replied. 'Methinks they are all deceased. Or, as you say in plain terms, "gone to heaven", to quote the eloquent Hamlet once again.'

'Waal, we'll leave it to the Lord to sort 'em out.' Luke glanced around through narrowed eyes. 'You sure they're all through? Where's Cameron.'

'Yonder.' Alphonse pointed a finger as Brad

Cameron whipped his horses and his buggy raced on two wheels around a corner and headed out of town at a gallop. 'He seems to be in a hurry.'

Luke raised his Sharps and sent a bullet whistling after the banker but he was soon out of range, just a dust cloud on the trail. 'King Rat seems to have deserted his ship. How about Sally?'

'Oh my God, yes,' Alphonse cried. 'She's alone at the cabin.' He climbed up on to the wagon box and yelled, 'We've no time to lose.' He released the brake and flicked the reins and the mule wasted no time in starting out of town in the opposite direction to Cameron's.

'I've an idea where it is,' Alphonse shouted back. 'Along at the mine at Cameron Creek. A modest monomaniac, wasn't he, named everything after himself.'

'Keep this wagon rolling.' Luke stifled his pain, clutching his jolted knee as he lay in the back. 'We ain't got no time to lose. All I pray is we're in time.'

Nelson Eades was a loose-limbed young man, with cadaverous features. He hadn't had much of a deal out of life. Everybody had treated him like a pariah-dog until Mr Cameron came along and put some cash in his poke. The only women he'd ever known were two-bit whores in saloons. So he had enjoyed treating Sally Roberts like one, dragging her around the cabin by her hair; ripping her clothes from her, slapping her about, taking his revenge for all those blows he had been handed out. But she wouldn't talk and, although Mr Cameron had cautioned him not

114

to go too far, he was getting desperate.

'Come on, gal,' he crooned, as he started on her again, slamming her back on to the cabin table, thrusting himself between her thighs. 'There ain't gonna be no more playing about. You're for the high jump.'

'Yeah, 'bout time too.' The other man Jimmy, had unbuttoned his flies and snarled. 'We been too soft on you, beautiful. You gonna git a mouthful of this.'

'OK,' Sally gasped. 'Take it easy boys. We don't have to be enemies. You be nice to me, I'll be nice to you.'

For days she had been trying to wheedle her way into Eades' affections, whispering to him that they could go away, be a twosome, that she really liked him. The man, Jimmy, was a different matter. There was no way she could soften him. A man with dead eyes and a heart of stone.

Suddenly the distant sound of shooting reverberated through the canyons towards them. 'What in hell's that?' Nelson jumped, reaching for his sixgun, poised over her.

'Sounds like some shoot-out back at town,' Jimmy said. 'Maybe we better go investigate?'

'No. First I'm having her.' He struggled to hold the desperately wriggling girl. 'She's been tauntin' and temptin' us fer days. We're gonna give it her 'fore we go no-place, eh, Jimmy.'

'Yeah, too right.' The older men shoved himself into her face. 'Wagh!' He leapt back, dancing and roaring like an irate grizzly as blood fountained from his private parts. 'The bitch bit me.'

115

Suddenly there was the rushing of wheels on the rocky ground outside, the neighing and stomping of the mule. 'What's that?' Nelson cried. 'Chris'sakes, Jimmy, quit that wailing.'

He dropped the girl's legs, pulled himself together, grabbed his carbine, and went to the cabin door, opening it a crack and peeping out. The tubby Alphonse was sat on the box of a wagon. Nelson stepped out. 'Yeah, whadda ya want?'

'There's trouble in Cameron. The boss says come quick, you and Jimmy, and bring the girl,' Alphonse cried. 'Is she OK?'

'Sure, she's OK. You go back and tell him we'll be on our way. Right now we're busy.'

'Where's Jimmy?'

'He's had a . . . accident. He ain't feelin' too good.'

'Call him out and bring the girl. There's no time to lose. That's an order from Cameron.'

Suddenly Sally, half-naked, bruised and bleeding, burst out of the cabin door, but Nelson caught her by her hair and put his carbine to her head, pulling her into him. 'Oh, no, not so fast. You git your wagon out of here, mister, or I'll kill this bitch. She and I are goin' places.'

'Don't be stupid, Nelson, my dear boy.' Alphonse scratched at his throat and slipped his pudgy hand inside his coat. 'Really, it's too hot for all this. Let her go.'

'We ain't letting nobody go.' Jimmy staggered out of the door, hugging a blanket between his legs. 'If he don't kill her I will. Look what she done to me.' He waved a revolver, wildly, cocking it to fire at the girl, when a slug whapped out from the side of the wagon sending him tumbling against the cabin wall.

'What the—?' Nelson Eades turned his carbine on to the wagon and fired but there was the whang of a ricochet as his lead met iron. 'Whass goin' on?'

'You asked for this, Nelson.' Alphonse tugged out his Luger. 'Farewell, my friend.'

Before he could return fire, the bullet sent Eades staggering back to join Jimmy in a twitching, bloody, useless pile on the ground. 'Alas,' Alphonse said, thudding in more slugs. 'I knew them so well.'

He jumped down and put an arm around the distraught girl. 'Don't cry, sweet maiden, you are safe now.'

Luke hauled himself up once more and studied her. 'You OK? Or is that a stupid question?'

'Yes, I'm OK.' She forced a smile as her tears began to flow. 'Are you?'

'Sure. Everythang's under control. We've wiped out that nest of rats. But I was asking you.'

'Yeah. I'll be all right.' She shuddered as the 'drummer' held her tight. 'I held them off. I thought just now it was the end for me. And then you turned up. Thank you.'

'Come on,' Alphonse said, 'let's get you back to town. I'll make you a nice hot toddy.'

'Before we go' – Luke pointed a finger at him – 'just who in hell are you?'

'I happen to work for the Federal Bureau of Investigation,' Alphonse announced, sliding the Luger back into his shoulder holster. 'I've been waiting for a colleague but I fear he has been delayed, possibly permanently.'

'You' – Luke grinned – 'you came to investigate Cameron and he gave you a job in his own bar?'

'Yerse, I thought the emolument he paid extremely weak. Did you like my act?'

'You betcha, pal. You even fooled me.'

ELEVEN

The town photographer was at work under his black cloth, with his big box camera on its tripod, taking pictures of Cy Cooper and The Hunter who were propped up on a board against the sidewalk.

'There's a government bounty of five hundred dollars on Cooper,' Alphonse said to Luke Hackman as they stood among the excited men, women and children who had come from their homes to rubberneck at the bloody aftermath of battle. 'You shot him so it will be coming to you.'

'How about the 'breed?'

'No, there ought to have been, but the law around here has been extremely lax in examining his activities.'

The body of his fellow federal agent had been brought in and he, too, was photographed for identification in Washington. 'I'll give my erstwhile colleague a decent send-off, but the others can go in a communal hole. If those villains have any kin no doubt they will be relieved to see the back of them.'

'I guess they were just drifters trying to make a

dollar or two,' Luke drawled. 'The flotsam of the great South West. Meanwhile, the main man has got away. What are you going to do about him?'

'Cameron's whole entrepôt I have put in escrow,' Alphonse announced. 'The Cameron ranch, the saloon, bank, store, copper mine at Cameron Creek, the whole shebang, all assets will be frozen, I have the authority and will act as third party. I've already seen his lawyer, Mr Harris, who tells me some phoney will has been drawn up bequeathing everything to a Mr McGinty, care of Nogales, undoubtedly Cameron's new pseudonymn.'

'Nogales, eh. That's just south of the border, ain't it? You got any kick down there?'

'Not strictly, but Diaz's government is wooing international support for his corrupt regime and his minions might turn a blind eye if I pull the right strings.'

'You mean you're gonna go down there and try to arrest him? I'll give you something, Alphonse, you've got some gall.'

'My colleague has been murdered, all these people have been killed. It is my duty to bring the man responsible to justice.' Alphonse removed his stovepipe hat and mopped his balding brow. 'You understand this is all *entre nous*, my dear boy. My intuition tells me to trust you. Why don't you come along for the ride?'

'Oh, no,' Luke protested. 'I ain't got no plans to go to Mexico. I'm heading for San Francisco. There's a big game coming up in October. There's some high rollers goin' to be playing and I'm gonna be in there.

Who knows, I might scoop top prize. Poker champion of all-America. It's been a dream of mine for some while. At least to try.'

'You've got two months to spare. Come on, Mr Hackman, resuscitate your leg for a couple of weeks and take a gamble on Mexico. There's a thousand bounty on Cameron. Just think of that. We can go by stage, if you like. My department picks up the bill, but I'm afraid I can only offer you five cents a mile, plus ammunition gratis. Be my friend, I need someone to side me.'

'Yeah, I guess you do, but it ain't gonna be me.'

'Are you sure about that?' Alphonse nudged him and smiled sweetly. 'Nogales is a wide-open border town. Gambling night and day. Think of all those doe-eyed *señoritas* who flock there to sell their favours for a few pesos. Aren't you into that kind of gay abandon? Regard it as a holiday.'

'Some holiday,' Luke growled, in his deep voice. 'He'll have enlisted another gang of *viciosos* by the time we – I mean, you – arrive. What chance you got of getting to him?'

'They would treble with a man like you alongside. I'm not joking. Think it over.'

'I've already told you. You deaf or somethang? – No. N–O. You got that, Alphonse? Or are you dumb, too?'

The tubby Federal man, in his flamboyant costume, climbed up on to a barrel on the sidewalk, cupped his mouth, and hollered, 'People of Cameron City, hear me. Your town has been rid of its corrupt rule. Cameron's gang has been routed and he is on the run. By the power invested in me by the Federal authorities I am going to arrange for the election of a new judge, mayor and sheriff. Cast your votes wisely. From henceforth Cameron City will become a decent, law-abiding, hard-working community where you folks can raise your families in peace and prosperity. Before I go might I suggest that an excellent candidate for sheriff of this town and county would be the man who has done so much to give you your freedom – Luke Hackman here. Give him a big hand, ladies and gents.'

'No way. I'm not interested. I'm a gambler not a lawman.' Luke raised his arm to the cheering crowd and limped on his Sharps into the Golden Eagle assisted by Ruby. 'What's that roly-poly li'l gofer think he's playin' at? He's jokin' if he thinks I've any plans about stayin' in this one-horse town. I shoulda been on my way a week ago. Gimme a shot of that bourbon, Ruby. I guess I've earned it.'

Ruby went behind the bar as he propped himself on a stool. 'Sure, Brad said it was on the house for you. Here's mud in your eye, *Sheriff.*'

'Cut the crap.' Luke tossed back the fiery spirit and pushed the glass back for a refill. 'How's the gal?'

'I've put her to bed and the doc's seen her. She'll be OK. She's a spunky kid.'

'She sure is. Some good-looker, too. An all-American gal.'

'Yes.' Ruby regarded him, sadly, and said in her husky voice as she lit a cigarette and sipped her own drink, 'I've noticed your interest in that little lady.'

'Aw,' he grinned. 'It's just fatherly.'

'You know, Luke, you oughta think about settling down. You ain't gettin' no younger. We got the railroad from California to Tucson coming through. Soon it'll be pushing on down into Mexico. Things are goin' to liven up in this territory. There's worse places to be. At least we don't get no snow. What you wanna go north for?'

'Not you, too, Ruby. Look, I allus been like the tumblin' tumbleweed. I just gotta keep movin' on. Thass the way I am. You know, one favour you could do me 'fore I go?'

'What's that?'

'Contact them two ranchers who cleaned me out. Arrange for a return game. You and me, I'm sure we can beat 'em. We would be playing a straight pack, no spyholes in the ceiling this time.'

Ruby smiled widely at him as she scraped her fingers back through her dark mane of hair. 'I'll do that, Luke. You an' me, we'll make a good partnership, huh?'

'Maybe. I just wanna beat those bozos fair and square. And I got nuthin' else to do for a coupla weeks. I'm stuck here 'til this leg heals.'

She smiled. 'That's good to hear.'

'Yeah.' He grinned at her, amiably. 'But I'll be boardin' at the widow's so I git some peaceful sleep. There is one thing I want to do, send a cable to my folks back in Texas.'

'Goodness gracious.' Alphonse had joined them, removing his lemon gloves. 'I never imagined you would be the filial type.'

123

'It'll be the first time I contacted 'em in ten years. My ole man used to larrup the shit outa me with the buckle end of his belt. That was 'til I growed up and smashed him in the jaw one day. I walked out and I ain't been back since. But there's somethang I need to know.'

'What's that, might I enquire?'

Luke shrugged. 'It's personal. A family thang. What's your poison, Alphonse? Or are you gonna fix us Manhattans? I guess it's time to celebrate.'

'Yerse, indeed.' Alphonse went behind the bar and fluttered his fingers as he selected bottles. 'That might well be in order, Mr Hackman. For order has been restored to this town.'

There was one other thing Luke Hackman wanted to do before he quit Cameron City. He borrowed some crutches from Doc Blount and hopped over to the gun shop. He purchased a goodly amount of dynamite and propelled himself, one-footed, along the trail out of town through the morning silence, no sign of life except for basking lizards among the rocks and cactus. When he reached the Chavez small-holding, lying back off the trail in a tree-hung decliv-ity, once a fertile little farm, now desolate and dry, its once-sturdy plants dying from lack of irrigation, he paused, and climbed down a narrow path to the adobe shacks that housed the families. '*Hola*!' he called.

They greeted him in an apathetic manner, a look of despair etched on their dark faces, even the chil-dren sad and solemn. Without their menfolk, with-

124

out water, how could they survive? '*Buenas*,' Isabella said, coming to the door of her *casa*. 'It is good to see you looking well again.'

'Yeah, well, in a coupla weeks time I hope to be able to say the same about you. Come with me. Show me where Cameron's men built that dam.'

They walked together up the dried river bed, the children and sisters-in-law following from a distance, until they reached the great pile of jumbled rocks through which a trickle of water seeped. 'Stand back,' he shouted to them, and knelt to stuff sticks of dynamite in the cracks, then lit the fuses. After that he hopped out of the way as fast as his crutches would carry him.

There was a mighty roar and Luke was thrown off his feet and tossed twenty paces forward by the blast of the explosion. It didn't do his leg much good, but he landed in a sandy spot, and when he looked round it was a sight for sore eyes. The Cameron river was pouring through the cracks in the dislodged rocks and resuming its natural course, flowing towards the allotments and wells of the Chavez clan in a frothing, bubbling surge. Soon it would settle back into its normal life-giving flow.

Isabella pulled him to his feet, found his crutches for him, and planted a deep-felt kiss on his lips, hugging him. '*Gracias*, Hackman, *muchas gracias*. You save my family. You save our farm. We will be always in your debt.'

Wine, tequila, food, and relatives appeared from far afield, and they began to dance and carouse to the music of guitar, flute and drums, making celebration as only Mexicans knew how. Luke was garlanded with leaves and flowers, regaled with food and drink, the hero of the hour. Isabella wanted him to dance but he begged out on account of his bad leg. '*Americano*,' Isabella called, 'we will be forever grateful to you.'

Her mother, Rosa, nudged him. 'She would make you a good wife. You would be welcome here.'

Luke shrugged and raised his hands. 'Aw, thass good of you but I ain't the marryin' kind. I gotta be on my way. I'm a lonesome gambler an' thass what I'll always be.'

Two weeks passed before the gambler felt that his leg was strong enough to ride. But first, he borrowed the widow's light rig and pony and called at the hotel to see Sally. She, too, had made a good recovery, her bruises and scratches faded, only the scars of her ordeal left in her mind.

'What's the matter?' she asked. 'Why are you staring at me?'

'You took my breath away.' He took off his Stetson, handing her into the surrey. 'I never thought to see you looking so fresh and lovely.'

Sally smiled her appreciation of the compliment. She had brushed her hair until it shone like summer corn, and bought a new dress of blue shantung which heightened the sparkling blue of her eyes. 'Where are we going?'

'We'll take a ride out to Cataract Creek.' He gave a flick of the whip. 'It's good to be out and about, ain't it?'

126

'It certainly is.' The breeze ruffled her hair as they clipped along the trail and she put an arm into his to steady herself on the fragile seat. 'You don't mind, do you?'

'Be my guest. It feels good.'

'I love this country.' They were passing the great monoliths that lined the canyons of the rushing creek. 'It's so . . . so cataclysmic.'

'Or, as Alphonse might say, Cyclopean.' He grinned at her and pulled in the pony to sit admiring the view. 'Hey, who's this coming? Looks like the ghost of a Johnny Reb.'

The soldier's uniform was not grey but smothered by the dust of travel. He introduced himself as Captain Tommy Byrne, of the Third US cavalry. 'I'm out of Fort Mojave. Thought I'd take a gander at Hualpai country.' He spoke with a strong Irish burr, shaking his head. 'It's a terrible shame how a once-dreaded tribe, who gave Uncle Sam such loyal service, has been left to live on the verge of starvation. They've been fearfully demoralized, especially the women.'

'Why's that?' Sally asked.

'Well, Miss, if I may be indelicate, it's the fault of the whiskey peddlers, the curse of this land. To get their hands on a bottle the squaws have posed naked for pictures that are then sold to the miners and railroad workers. The braves, too, have gone down, slaves to whiskey and gambling.'

'It is a terrible thing,' Sally agreed. 'I know first-hand.'

'The young lady's a widow. Her husband was a

127

drinker and gambler. You can't combine the two.'

'In that case, ma'am, might I venture that you are well rid of him. I don't mean to sound cruel, but if he went on that way it could only have ended in calamity.'

'I don't know.' Sally sighed, wistfully. 'Billy was not that bad. But I suppose there's some truth in what you say.'

She tried to change the subject, smiling brightly. 'Why don't you share our picnic with us?'

She took her box hamper and they found a spot looking out over the canyon to sit and eat the chicken lunch and pies she had prepared. A huge condor, with its nine-foot wingspan, suddenly alighted on the cliff-edge to join them.

Sally tossed it a bit of chicken skin. 'It's odd how it's so ugly at close hand, waddling around, with its red and yellow head, and so awesome when it drifts on the currents out there.'

'Sure, it's being shot to pieces, like the coyotes,' Byrne remarked. 'It'll be extinct soon. People blame it for taking calves and sheep, like they blame the coyotes. Their predations are greatly exagerrated. It's a shame. It don't do much harm. The coyotes mainly eat insects, grubs, mice and garter snakes. They are being killed and poisoned by their thousands. That's another grievance for the Hualpais for they have always worshipped the coyote as a god, man's chief friend and bringer of fire, though how he did that I ain't so sure.'

When the trooper got back on his army plug and was about to leave, Sally called, 'It's been interesting talking to you, Captain Byrne.'

'Ach, I never regarded the redman solely as an enemy. They were good people, badly treated. But it's all over now.'

They stood and waved goodbye, and Luke slipped his arm around the girl's waist as they watched the lowering sun paint the great canyons shades of ochre and vermilion.

'Hold me for a minute, Luke,' she whispered. 'Make me feel safe.'

He hugged her to him and kissed her lips. When he broke apart he said, 'That was by way of goodbye. I'll be leaving in the morning.'

'What?' She clung to him. 'For California?'

'No. I'm going after Cameron.' He pulled a letter from his pocket. 'You'd better look at this. You know I sent a cable back to Texas. This is what the old man had been keeping from me.'

His cable to George Hackman, Fort Worth, had read:

PA STOP IMPORTANT TO KNOW WHO WAS TRUE FATHER STOP DID I HAVE BROTHER? STOP PLEASE REPLY POST OFFICE CAMERON CITY ARIZONA STOP LUKE.

In reply had come a letter reading:

'Dear Luke,
It was a surprise to hear from you out of the blue since you ran off all them years ago. Your beloved, adoptive mother, my wife Mary, passed

over into the Vale of Shadows only weeks ago and I hope this news brings a tear to your eye. Pray for her soul as she always prayed for yours. I tried to thrash some Christian duty into you, boy, but it seems you are still involved in your harum-scarum, whoring, gambling ways. You never would buckle down. Your brother, Seth, and his wife, help me run the store. Maybe I favoured him at times over you but I guess that was only natural as he is my true son and is now a decent, honest man. You ask about your true father. He was a man named Ethan Jones. He and his wife farmed in the village of Shiloh before its fine orchards became a bloody battle-ground. Forty thousand soldiers lost their lives there in two days, but also civilians died. The Jones's house was flattened by a shell. Ethan died instantly. His wife, Elizabeth, died in child-birth. Her twin boys survived. One of them was you. Your mother and I out of charity adopted you. Another Kentucky farmer, Bill Cameron, raised the other boy, Bradley. Out of curiosity I once wrote to Bill to ask what had happened to him. Apparently his boy, too, was wild like you, ran off from home and went to the bad down in Memphis. As you know, because you came with us, aged three, after the war I moved with my regiment to Fort Worth for frontier duties. When I was invalided out with Comanche arrowheads still in my chest Mary and I opened the store. You never took to Bible-reading, or doing anything useful around the house to help out. Soon as you were fourteen all you thought about was playing cards and chasing girls. Maybe, on our jaunts out hunting, I did teach you some Indian tricks, survival skills that have served you, or possibly saved you, out in that wild country of the Arid Zone. When you was a youngster I thought it best to withold this information of your true parentage from you and raise you as my own. But these things will out and I hope the knowledge satisfies you. It may also interest you to know that your ex-wife, Pauline, who you treated so shabbily, has married a God-fearing Temperance man and they live happily with their three children in Yokum. So you can forget her. Well, we all join in sending you our best wishes. Take care, you scallawag.

Yours sincerely, your one-time Pa,
George (Hackman).

'Goodness!' Sally blinked as she scrutinized the letter. 'What a surprise this must be for you.'

'Not really. When I first met Brad Cameron it was like looking in a mirror, but at someone else. Not just his similar image, something deeper that disturbed me. We'd only met once before, at birth, but it was as if I'd known him all my life.'

'Two sides of a coin. The good and the bad.'

'Don't think of me as the good. I've committed my share of misdemeanours. It looks like we've both gone to the bad.'

'You're not bad, Luke. Not like him. He's truly

evil, the amount of suffering he's caused. He may not have pulled the trigger himself, but how many people have been killed or had their lives ruined because of him?'

'Yeah. That's why I gotta stop him. I'm gonna bring him in, Sal. Or try to. He's gonna have to face up to what he's done.'

'Luke.' She caught hold of his arm as he tucked the letter away. 'Be careful. He might be your twin, but he's not the same as you. Even if he knows you're his brother, if it serves his purpose he will killl you, too.'

'Yeah? Well it looks like us Jones boys are going to have to have this out.'

TWELVE

Not many years before it would have been a brave man who ventured to traverse Arizona Territory from the Colorado Canyon in the north to the southern line established by the Gadsen Purchase, a desolate land infested by bloodthirsty Apaches, who had scared most of the population out of their wits, put *ranchos* to the flames, tortured, raped, slaughtered and run off thousands of settlers, in an area the size of Germany where the savage had reigned supreme. And all because the white men's treaties had, as they said, been written in sand.

But in the mid-1880s, it was a different picture. The tribes had been defeated and relocated. The mines and bull-trains were back in business, trade and industry were thriving in the far-flung towns.

Alphonse Strudl and Luke Hackman made good time riding their horses past the towering San Francisco peak, capped with snow in summer and winter, through Flagstaff and the army post of Camp Verde, following the Rio Verde to its confluent with the Gila River that cuts the territory cross-wise in half.

There lightning flickered and thunder rumbled as the heavens opened and the rains of the summer solstice bucketed down. On they tramped to Fort Grant and followed the winding trail that descended to the mile-wide bottomlands of Tucson encircled by the mountain ranges of the Santa Catalinas, the Baboquivari Peak, The Santa Ritas, and the Superstitions, with not far away the murky, forbidding ranges of Old Mexico.

'How the hell did I git talked into this?' Luke asked, as rain tipped from his hat brim and runnelled down his neck, and his skewbald floundered through the quagmire which was Tucson's main street. 'I need my brain testing.'

'Well, we could have rode in comfort on the stage but you insisted on bringing that nag.' Alphonse looked about him as they passed the church of San Antonio, the piles of rubbish on the sides of the street, the *burros*, horses and carriages left abandoned in the mud as their owners sought refuge in saloons, restaurants and gambling halls. 'At least they've built a hotel since I was last here so we can rest our bones under cover for once.'

He descended awkwardly from his mustang, stiffly climbed the slippery wooden steps to the Paradise Hotel, flapped water from his frock coat, removed his Lincoln hat and announced, 'These wet saddles play havoc with one's piles. Will I not be glad to return to civilization when this assignment is through?'

'Ach, come off it, Alphonse, you're loving every minute of your sojourn in the great West.' Luke

134

bonged the desk bell for the clerk and booked them into a room. 'Looks like I gotta share a bed with you tonight. That should be a thrill.'

'It's all we have left, sir,' the clerk warbled. 'If you'd care to sign the book.'

Luke did so and studied the scribbled page. 'Who's this? Hiram McGinty? Was he a big fella, a tad like me? When was he here?'

'There's the date, sir. That would be two weeks back. He only stayed one night.'

'Where was he headin'? Did he say?'

'I've no idea,' the clerk replied. 'We don't acquaint ourselves with our client's business, only his welfare.'

'Yeah?' Luke looked about him at a tattered horse-hair sofa, a threadbare rug and wobbly pine furniture. A glass-eyed, moth-eaten moose peered down at them from his wall bracket. 'You coulda fooled me. Come on, Alphonse, let's stash our gear and go find a livery for the broncs. They deserve a feed after carrying us two heavyweights four hundred miles.'

'He's got a good start on us,' Alphonse sighed as they clomped up the stairs and pushed into one of the pine-board partitioned cubicles. 'Ooh, dear, it's a bit cramped in here.'

'Never mind, sweetheart,' Luke grinned, dumping his saddle, pack and carbine. 'It's only for one night.' He took a pack of cards from his pocket and skimmed through it. 'Anyway, don't expect me back too early. Didn't you hear that roulette wheel clicking as we passed the casino?'

*

135

In the morning they passed the imposing domes of the red adobe church at San Xavier del Bac, where converts to Catholicism, Papagoe Indians, worshipped in their fashion. They clipped on their way another hundred miles to Tubac, passing double wagons of iron pilings, pulled by teams of twenty mules, going south, and *caretas* from Sonora loaded with fruit, spices and salad goods heading north to Tucson. Trade sure was booming.

'Welcome to Mexico,' Alphonse called, as they left the United States and sauntered their steeds into the dirty and dishevelled border town of Nogales. He touched his hat to a group of *rurales* who sprawled at rickety tables outside a *cantina* taking their ease, sombreros the size of cartwheels, the brims weighed down with silver conchos, protecting them from the harsh sun.

'Smile sweetly at these scum of the prisons who keep *El Presidente* in power. They are the ones we have to woo.'

The *rurales*, in their tight uniforms, strung with bandoleers of bullets, their scarlet-lined capes slung over chair backs, gave gap-toothed sneers and laughed evilly, as the two gringos passed by, Luke flicking his fingers to them. Most men dared not meet their eyes.

'Yeah, they look a jolly bunch. I've a feeling we're gonna have a high ole time in this place.'

It was a bustling town and a hustling town. Luke had the feeling that everybody was involved in some nefarious enterprise. A mixture of clapboard saloons, whorehouses, stores and cheap hotels, was

136

surrounded by a shanty town of one-storey adobes or brush jacals, set down on a wide plain to mark an artificial line that separated two countries, two cultures. Apart from the babble of marketeers and street vendors, the main occupation appeared to be the exchange of currency, the sale of guns and stolen property, and attempts to part the gringos from their dollars.

'Hey, meester.' A small boy tugged at Luke's chaps as soon as he swung down from his skewbald. 'You wan' my seester? Ver' good, ver' cheap, *señor*. Come you follow me.'

'No thanks, sonny. But I'll give you fifty cents if you keep an eye on my hoss while I'm in this establishment. If anybody looks him over you come quick and let me know.' He translated this into frontier Castilian. 'He and I are old pals, you see. We don't wanna be parted.'

'Isn't that inviting him to steal it?' Alphonse asked as they stepped into a drinking den.

'No, I think most Mexicans are pretty honest underneath. They jest get corrupted in towns like these.' Luke pointed to a cask propped on the dirt floor. 'From now on I ain't drinkin' the water. It's tequila for me.' He took a bite of a piece of lemon, a lick of salt between thumb and finger and slugged back the contents of an earthenware mug. 'Whoo!' he gasped. 'Sheepherder's delight. Try it, Alphonse. They don't serve Manhattans in these parts.'

'Jesus!' Alphonse choked as he tried a stone beaker-full. 'What is it? Pure cactus juice?'

There was a smoky aroma of burning pigskin on a

brazier. Luke paid for two portions and took a bite of his, crunching the fatty gristle in his teeth. 'Seems to be their favourite repast in these parts, apart from fried grasshoppers.'

'Excuse me if I refrain,' Alphonse squeaked, waving his proferred portion away.

There was another tug at Luke's trousers and the small boy was staring up at him, serious-faced. 'Man look at your horse,' he said.

Luke shrugged, and strode to the bead-curtained doorway, parting it, to peer through. An *Americano*, by his clothes, had a hand on the skewbald's rump and was assessing its brand, the heavy Denver saddle and carbine in the boot. He was an average-looking Joe, in dusty pants and boots, vest and low-crowned hat, with a heavy moustache. He wore crossed gunbelts with a revolver slung on each thigh, another small-arm stuck in his belt. He glanced at the drinking dive and hurried away. Luke followed him, pushing through the crowds.

The heavily-armed *hombre*, who, like Luke, stood head and shoulders above most of the native population and thus was not difficult to follow, led him unwittingly, unaware that he was being followed, to the *cantina* where the surly-looking gang of *rurales* were roistering, strode through them and went inside.

Luke stood back in the shade of a building and looked across as Alphonse came puffing up to join him. 'Some hard-head was looking at my horse. I figure he's gone in there to report. But I don't fancy my chances getting past those *rurales*. I got a hunch

Cameron might be in there.'

'We could get in round the back.'

'I could take a look. You stay here.'

'No, I'll provide you with a diversion at the front. I'll have a little chat with our *rurale* friends.'

'I ain't sure that's wise, Alphonse. Those bozos ain't nice to know.'

'Don't you worry about me. You go, see what you can see. Cameron must be here someplace. Think of the bounty on him. Dead or alive. Wait, I'll go first.'

Luke watched as Alphonse, in his top hat and frock coat, waddled across towards the *cantina*. Two of the *rurales* gave contemptuous guffaws as Alphonse paused before them, doffed his hat with a theatrical flourish, and appeared to engage them in conversation.

'He's got a nerve, that guy,' Luke murmured. 'Cool as a cucumber.'

He tugged his own hat-brim down and strolled across the street, slipping into an alleyway at the side of the two-storey *cantina*. He stepped over a box of mouldy melons, peered around the corner and made his way past a noisy kitchen to another door-way. As was the custom in Arizona there was no lock on the wooden door, only a log propped against it to keep it secure. He kicked it aside and slid into a dark-ened interior.

Luke was waiting for his eyes to get accustomed to the gloom when he heard a rustling in the straw covering the floor and a girl's voice pleaded, 'Please, mister, help me.'

He took a match from a tin box in his pocket and

struck it on his thumb. By its flickering light he saw the wide, lucent eyes of a teenage girl. She was hog-tied, her wrists pulled behind her and bound to her ankles with rawhide which was looped tight around her throat.

'What you doing here?' he asked, somewhat fool-ishly, before he recalled that one of the biggest contra-bands that passed through Nogales was kidnapped females, both American and Latino. They would be sold on further into Mexico to rich *haciendados* for their private harems, or forced to work in brothels. When they got too old they would be used as slave labour in the silver mines. 'Hey, this don't look good.'

He lit another match and saw two older women, similarly trussed, one thin, auburn-haired, with freckly white skin, the other olive-complexioned and dumpy. Their clothes were torn, they were scratched and bruised, and fear was etched on their faces as they regarded him. 'Ssh!' He put a finger to his lips. 'I ain't gonna hurt you.'

'Why are you doing this to us?' the young girl cried. 'Have you no pity?'

'I ain't doin' nuthin' to you. It ain't my business.'

'But, you, you were upstairs. You . . . you. . . .'

'What? There's a guy looks like me upstairs? Good, thass just the man I'm lookin' for. Where you from, kid?'

'Tucson. I was on the stage to Fort Yuma. They stopped it, robbed and killed the others, dragged me here. They did terrible things to me.'

'Yeah, I can guess,' Luke huskily whispered. 'How about you, lady?'

'They raided our *rancho*, snatched me when my husband was away. I'm Kathleen Gallagher. This is my servant, Maria. Mister, you gotta do something, get out word to the Rangers.'

'You're in Mexico now, honey. The Rangers won't venture this far.'

'Oh, God! Are we in Mexico? We were blindfolded, smuggled in under a wagonload of corn. They sold us to that man upstairs. What's he going to do with us?'

'Lady, I hate to think. Sell you on at a considerable profit is my guess.'

There was the sound of talking and laughter outside the kitchen door and the crunch of boots coming towards them. The door was hauled open as Luke stepped back into the shadows, easing out his Remington. The *hombre* he had followed stepped inside and knelt down beside the teenage girl, stroking her cheek.

'Hey, how ya doin'?' he asked, staring at her, after giving the other two only a cursory glance. 'You know your trouble? You're too damn pretty. When they put you up on that block you gonna fetch a helluva price.'

'Please,' the girl whimpered, 'don't hurt me.'

'I ain't gonna hurt ya. Aw, we was a bit rough, I know, earlier on. But you didn't mind, did ya? How about I release your ropes, let you stretch them lovely legs of yourn? You'd like that, wouldn't ya? We gotta hit the trail tonight. We're headin' for the Valley de Suya. It's gonna be a bumpy ride. But, 'fore then you need to relax, honey. Come on now' – he started to unknot the ropes around her ankles – 'we gonna have us some fun. Only, don't you go blabbin' to McGinty upstairs, or cryin' out, or I'll have to give ya a whack. You see, you're s'posed t'be in prime condition, gal, a virgin, no less. Heck!' – he grappled with her as her legs were released and she gasped out as he fell on her, groping at her clothing and trying to kiss her lips – 'A virgin! That's a laugh! Come on, you wildcat, I'm gonna give it you.'

'Says you, buddy,' Luke grunted, as he thunked his revolver butt across the top of his spine and the *hombre* slumped unconscious. The girl was shuddering uncontrollably. 'Come on, honey, you're gonna be OK.' He stroked her hair from her face. 'Look, ladies, I gotta go. I'll be back.'

THIRTEEN

'Where you theenk you go, gringo.' One of the *rurales*, a swarthy, paunchy individual, stuck his cavalry sword out across the gangway of the terrace as Alphonse Strudl tried to enter the *cantina*. 'This place only for *rurales*.'

'I humbly beg your pardon, sir. I was merely in pursuit of a little light refreshment.'

'Oh, yah?' The *rurale*'s gold-teeth glinted as he grinned at his pals wickedly. 'The fatguts gringo likes his grub.'

Another of the *rurales* jabbed Aphonse's posterior with his boot, growling, 'Where you from, *hombre*? Where you going?'

' "Sooth, sir, my determinate voyage is mere extravagancy." ' He touched fingers to his cravat and fluttered them daintily. 'Perhaps you're not familiar with *Twelfth Night*?'

'What's he say?' another scowled. 'He try to be funny?'

Others of the dozen *rurales* lounging at the terrace tables pricked up their ears. They were the lower step of the pyramid of power, above them the *federales*, the *haciendados*, the generals, the Catholic bishops, the rich and powerful who kept the Mexican populace in a state of fear and abject poverty, while President Diaz, in his palace, balanced at the top of the pyramid pretending to be the benevolent father to them all. The communists and socialists, the atheists and church-wreckers, had been suppressed. Mexico groaned under the first fascist police state of modern times.

The *rurales*, most of them thugs, murderers and felons, swaggered in their newfound authority. They were untouchable. They did only the bidding of their superiors. Or that of the men who bribed them best. And this new gringo, Señor McGinty, had arrived in Nogales and in a matter of weeks bought up saloons, brothels and gaming dens. Not only did the *rurales* get free drinks and free girls, but he was paying them well for their protection.

One of them winked at his brethren and stuck out his leg behind Alphonse. The first man, with a sergeant's chevrons on his sleeve, stood, and making a mincing motion of hands and hips, stepped close to the tubby American and gave him a sudden shove. Alphonse did a backward roll, his feet kicking the air.

The *rurales* roared with laughter as he picked himself up and brushed himself down. 'Your manners, gentlemen,' he said, amiably, 'could do with a little mending.'

Gringo-baiting was a bit of harmless fun to the *rurales*, but they regretted that the president had decreed that Americans, in general, should be

welcomed to their country, especially if they had
dollars to invest in cattle and mining. It prohibited
them shooting them out of hand – unless there was
just cause. But this impertinent little pipsqueak
looked like he might deserve to be beaten up and
thrown in jail. So they closed their chairs in around
Alphonse, blocking his escape, grinning at him.

'Your halitosis indicates a garlic breakfast, gentlemen.' Alphonse held his nose and fluttered his
fingers in obvious insult. The sergeant roared and
gave him another shove. He tumbled back and was
caught in the arms of a moustachioed corporal who
blammed his fist down on his hat. He hurled the
gringo back.

Alphonse recovered himself and stared sadly at his
concertinaed headpiece. 'Now really, this is too
much,' he said, and caught sight of Luke Hackman
at the far corner of the *cantina*, pointing his finger
towards the upper floor.

Alphonse gave a little wave and shouted, ' "If 'tis to
be done 'twere best it were done quickly".'

Luke stepped back into the cover of the wall and
returned to the back of the building. He strolled
casually through the kitchen door, doffed a hand to
the Mexican cooks, saw a staircase and started up it.
A big *rurale* was leaning against a wall at the top of
the landing outside a closed door. He had a rifle in
one hand and was picking his teeth with the finger of
another.

'What you want?' the guard asked in Spanish,
mumbling the words lazily. 'Uh – you – Señor
McGinty? I thought you inside office.'

145

'I ain't McGinty.' Luke gripped the rifle barrel and smashed it up under the guard's chin.

The big man yelped as he bit his finger. 'Ow!'

Luke cracked him with the rifle a second time, but harder, and the big man slid down the wall and slumped out for the count. The gambler took a deep breath, pulled out his Remington, cocked it with his thumb and kicked open the door.

Brad Cameron was sitting behind a desk, counting through a pile of greasy peso notes. He jerked his arms back to rest on his fingertips and stared at the intruder. For moments it was as if time stood still as the two brothers glared at each other.

Then Cameron snarled, 'You! What are you doing here?'

'I'm taking you back, Brad. You gotta face up to what you've done. You've been a bad boy, Brad. I figure you'll get life.'

'Are you joking? You think you're gonna waltz me outa here? The place is crawling with *rurales*. They're in my pay, goddamit. I only got to say the word and you're a dead man. And, come to think of it, that's just what I need. A fall guy.'

'Don't kid yourself, Brad. It's over. I got a Federal with me. You've had one of 'em killed, but you can't kill 'em all.'

'You? Why you doing this? What's it got to to do with you?'

'I got my reasons Brad. Ain't you guessed? Don't you know about us?'

'Us? What you yammering about? You crazy?'

'Yeah, I must be.' He stepped around the desk as

Cameron's hand slid towards a drawer. 'Oh, no.' He opened the drawer, removed the automatic pistol of newfangled design, stuffed it in his belt, and stuck the Remington hard into Cameron's neck. 'Come on, I'm taking you back alive. On your feet. Let's move.'

He guided Cameron by one arm across to a front window, smashed it with his elbow and hollered out, thrusting his twin forward: 'This man's my prisoner. I'm taking him back to America. You soldiers down there, put your weapons aside, don't try to interfere. I want no more killing.'

But the *rurales* were not used to such arbitrary dictates, nor had they much subtlety in their protection service. Their instinct was to scramble to their feet and go, excitedly, for their guns, smashing the window further with a fusillade of shots.

Luke jumped back as Cameron grinned. 'Don't seem like they want me to go, does it?'

Outside, the encircled Alphonse calmly took his Luger from his carpetbag, shot into the backs of three of the men who were blamming away with their weapons in front of him. He made a run for the door, turned and saw the swarthy sergeant aiming his carbine at him. 'Oh, you!' Alphonse pointed the Luger, squeezed the trigger, and the sergeant gawped as a bullet tore into his belly and sat him back in his seat.

Luke pushed Cameron out of the office to the top of the stairs. He heard a sound and looking along saw the guard, still on his backside, pulling back the bolt

147

of his rifle to fire. The Texan got his shot in first and the *rurale* collapsed.

Alphonse was beating off a volley of shots aimed at the door, but had to pause, crouching back, to reload, clacking a clutch of eight bullets up through the base of the Luger's butt. A Mexican cook had his machete raised about to hurl at him. Luke shot him and he fell face down into a tureen of soup.

'Enjoy your dinner,' Luke said, as he shoved Cameron slipping and sliding down the stairs before him.

Two more *rurales* had run to the back door and were charging in, their carbines blazing. Alphonse and Luke gave them a dose of biaxial firing and they went down like legless dummies. They jumped over them, dragging Cameron with them.

'You won't get away with this,' he roared.

'How much you bet?' Luke noticed a wagon with two horses standing already in the traces, probably in readiness to take the kidnapped women deeper into Mexico. 'Get him on it, Alphonse, and cover me.'

He dived back into the darkened room, as the man he had knocked unconscious came to and went for his gun. The bullet ripped his new shirt sleeve and he replied in kind, but more accurately. 'That's the last slug he'll ever shoot,' Luke muttered as he finished him.

He picked up the dead man's revolver and stuck his arm out the door firing at some more *rurales* who were running around the corner of the *cantina* trying to get a bead on Alphonse who had taken cover inside the wagon. They spun like tops and fell away.

Luke stuffed his empty Remington away, drew his knife and cut the women's bonds. 'Quick,' he shouted. 'Over to the wagon.'

The two older women were so stiff they could hardly walk so Luke had to drag and half-carry them. The girl was not in such a bad way as she had had her legs freed. She helped push them into the back of the covered wagon. And smiled at Luke as she climbed in herself. 'Thank you, *señor*.'

'Don't thank me. We ain't home yet.'

He ran around the side and jumped up on the box seat as Alphonse beat off the attack of more *rurales*. Luke grabbed a bull whip from its holder and cracked it over the ears of the horses, who started away, their ears flattened. 'Haaagh!'

The moustachioed corporal ran out before him, a revolver in his hand, shooting wildly at him. Luke sent the six-foot rawhide snake cutting across his arm and he dropped his gun like it was a hot brick.

'Haagh!' he shouted again as he sent the horses skittering along at the back of the houses and swung them through a narrow lane, scattering market vendors' stalls as they jumped for cover. He hauled the wagon back round into the main drag and sent it galloping. He glanced back and saw two more rurales running after them, firing their rifles. The bullets whistled too close for comfort.

'Go on! Haagh!' he shouted, and whipped the horses into a frenzy as they approached the customs barrier, going around the edge of waiting traffic, and crashing through the pole which snapped like a twig as the customs officers leaped for safety. 'Come on, go, you varmints!'

They were back on the US side of Nogales, but he kept the pair galloping through the main street and out on the trail to Tucson. In the back the women screamed as they hung on desperately, and Alphonse lay on the top of Cameron, his pistol to his head. 'There's a couple of *rurales* following,' he shouted.

'That must be about all the men they got left. You can take 'em, Alphonse.' He tossed Cameron's automatic back. 'Use this.'

The *rurales* on their mustangs gradually gained on the wagon, but Alphonse waited for them to close and, with his two-gun rearguard action, took one from his saddle. The other contented himself with hurling abuse and dropped back. He had had enough. He jumped down to his wounded comrade and watched them go.

They rested and watered the horses at Tubac, a nondescript town of boxy adobes and hitching rails both sides of a dusty street, more Mexican than American.

'It's OK,' Luke said, helping the girl, whose name was Melanie, and the two women down from the wagon. 'You're safe now. We'll soon be back in Tucson.'

Alphonse had tied Cameron's wrists in front of him, and prodded him from the wagon with the automatic. 'You can stretch your legs and have a drink with us. I'll read you your prisoner's rights. I'm taking you back to Memphis.'

They had pulled into the forecourt of a *cantina* and Luke went inside to rustle up three *gaseosas* and three beers. He came out bearing them on a tray.

Alphonse had absent-mindedly laid his reloaded Luger down on the table. Suddenly Cameron snatched it up with both bound hands, jumped back and pointed it at them. 'All right, hold it,' he growled, his eyes fierce. 'The ball's in my court now. We're gonna turn that wagon round and head back to where we came from. They gonna give you murderers of *rurales* a nice welcome in Nogales.'

'Mind if I have a drink 'fore I go?' Luke asked and placed the glasses on the table. He raised one and took a swig. 'Don't be a fool, Brad. This ain't gonna do no good.'

'You do what I say. Come on, I don't want no tricks. Any of you make a wrong move I'll shoot you down like dogs.'

'Hey,' Luke coaxed, backing away. 'Why don't we make this 'tween you and me? You reckon you could beat my draw? Or are you really the coward everybody knows you to be?'

Maybe it was the contemptuous way the women looked at him, or maybe something else, but Cameron faltered. 'First I'll take a drink of that beer,' he said, licking his dry lips, 'then we'll back off ten paces each. You keep your hands raised, Federal man, and keep out of this. You wimmin git outa the way. Girl! You come here, raise that glass to my lips and undo this rope round my wrists.'

He drank and was freed and stepped back. 'Right, now see if I'm scared or not. Gambler, or what's your name, Luke? Are you ready?'

'Sure.' The Texan's face tensed. 'Stick that gun in your belt. It'll be a fair draw.'

The two men faced each other and began to step away. At the tenth pace Cameron pulled the Luger free and aimed for a heart shot. But the safety catch was on and he fiddled, trying to release it. Luke Hackman brought out his Remington, deliberately raised it and aimed at his opponent's belt buckle. He gritted his teeth, squeezed the trigger and the gun barked flame. But the bullet spat into the dust by Cameron's boots.

Cameron stared at him as the Texan let the Remington swing loose. 'What'n hell's the matter with you? You coulda killed me easy.'

'How can I?' Luke shouted, his face pained. 'I'm your brother. Your twin brother. Ain't you guessed that yet?'

'My brother? Who you kidding?' But Cameron's look of disbelief turned to one of determination as he managed to release the safety and aimed the Luger at Hackman. 'Well, I don't give a damn about that. I'll see you in hell.'

Alphonse stood, his hands raised, helpless. 'Don't do it Cameron,' he pleaded. 'He spared you.'

Suddenly, a rider came charging down the street towards them. 'Hey, look who it ain't,' the former barkeep, Steve Fellowes, called out, whirling his mustang around, waving his Colt Thunderer revolver in his hand. 'Mister High-and-Mighty Cameron. Whadda ya know! I been waiting for this. Come on, you lousy stinking toerag. You've got your gun out. Try me.'

Cameron swung around and the Luger spat bullets, but Fellowes had whirled his mustang away. He came back around and fired his Thunderer double action point-blank, tumbling Cameron into the dust.

'Yee-ha!' Fellowes yelled. 'Revenge is sweet. And there's the lousy gambler who thinks he's so smart. This is my lucky day.' He slammed out another two shots at Luke, but his expression changed, the smile wiped off his face.

The Texan had knelt to one side and in return ploughed two bullets into Fellowes' abdomen. 'I ain't so sure about your lucky day,' he drawled as he watched the greasy-haired 'keep topple into the dust, blood seeping from his shirt. 'That perfume of yourn? What was it for? To hide your dogstink.'

'You rotten bastard.' Fellowes coughed blood and spoke no more.

Luke went across to his fallen brother who was staring at the blood gouging from his chest as if it was impossible that it could be happening to him.

'Thank Christ you got him for me,' he gritted out, looking up at the Texan. 'So you're my twin, eh?' He let the Luger fall into the dust and offered his hand. 'Well, nice to meetcha at this somewhat late stage. If you're my brother, why couldn't you have just let me go? I'd have been OK in Mexico.'

'I'm sorry, Brad. I couldn't. You've caused too much trouble and pain.'

'Yeah, I'm sorry, too.' Cameron hung on to his twin's hand. 'Maybe if we'd been raised different. If we'd been together.'

'It's too late now Brad. You're going fast.'

'Yeah, so long, gambling man. Try to have a better life than mine.' Cameron tried to force a grin, but he gave a jerk of his head and fell back, his eyes losing their light.

Luke closed them with his fingers and stayed on one knee for a while, staring at his dead brother. What thoughts went through his head he did not say. But he got up, blinked a tear from his eyes and said, 'I'll take him back to Tucson and bury him.'

Alphonse went over and picked up his Luger. 'That was careless of me. Still, it saves a lot of paper-work.'

Luke eyed him, suspiciously. 'Don't make me think you did that deliberately? Aw, hell!' He slapped the Federal man on his back. 'Come on, let's roll. It's over now.'

FOURTEEN

Harris, the lawyer, came into the Golden Eagle and said, 'Mr Hackman, you're' rich.'

Luke looked up from his game of blackjack. 'Yeah? Why?'

'Shall we have a private word or do you want the whole saloon to hear?'

'I'm easy. I ain't got nuthin' to hide.'

'Well, I've just been totting up the late Brad Cameron's assets. The Federals have taken a punitive one hundred grand but there's still over sixty-thousand dollars in various bank accounts, which have been released to the executor, that's me. Then there's this saloon and hotel, the bank, the emporium, his big cattle ranch next door to Isabella's place, various tracts of land and farms he bought up from the Latinos. In all, it's worth a fortune. All this was legally his. There's nothing the Feds can do about it.'

'Wow!' Luke shook his head and played his card. 'So, he was a rich man. What's that got to do with me?'

'Don't you see? You're his next of kin. It will all go to you.'

'You don't say? Right this moment I'm fifty dollars down on this pot and that's what worries me.'

Ruby slipped off her bar stool, swinging her rhine-stone necklace, swishing across in her worn and stained satin dress, plonking herself on Luke's knee. 'Hey, big boy.' She wound an arm around his neck and planted a kiss on his lips. 'You're rich, didn't you hear?'

'Yeah, sure. I'll believe that when I see it. You ever believed anything a lawyer says? There'll be a catch in it.'

'You're rich. It's true, ain't it, Mr Harris? Fifty dollars? It's peanuts to you. You'll be able to take me to San Francisco in style for that big poker conven-tion. We won't need any backers now. You ought to be buying everybody drinks on the house to cele-brate.'

'Sure.' He threw his hands in the air. 'Everybody have a drink. It's on me. OK? Now let's get on with this game.'

A cheer went up as all the men and girls rushed the bar to order their favourite tipple. 'Hang on a *momento*,' Alphonse cried. 'I've only got one pair of hands.' He had decided to retire from the Feds to stay on as dispenser of cocktails.

When the game finished, Luke rose from his seat, seventy dollars worse off. 'It's not my day,' he groaned, stretching.

'Mr Hackman, I'll be needing your signature on several documents,' Harris pressed. 'It's imperative the bank re-opens if this town is to stay solvent.'

'Alphonse,' Luke shouted, 'gimme a bourbon. You know anythang about running a bank?'

Alphonse made a face, and Gallicly shrugged. '*Un petit peu, peut être.*'

'Right, it's yours.'

'Gee, thanks.'

'Ruby, could you manage this gaming establishment?'

'Sure, better than Brad did.'

'Good, you take over tonight and run it while I'm away at San Francisco. If you make a profit by the time I return you'll get top salary and a cut.'

'Honey,' she purred, huskily, 'I thought I was coming with you.'

'There's been a change of plans. Sorry to disappoint you, but I'm gettin' married. I'm expecting her on the stage tonight.'

'Married? You two-timing twister. Who?'

'Don't get mad. I ain't made you no promises. You and me can still be good partners. You'll do well out of it. Hell, I wish I could be like an Apache and have four wives, but it ain't allowed in our puritan white Christian civilization.'

'Which four?' Ruby demanded.

'Well, the widow, to mend my socks, wash my shirts, make me a nice bed and apple pie. Isabella, to run the ranch and because she's a great lady, but I hear she's got a solid Mex fella lined up so that's out. You, Ruby, to play a natty round of cards and relax with in a saucy manner. And fourth ... hey!' He heard the sound of wheels as the stage from Flagstaff came rushing in. 'Here she is, I hope.'

Hank Wiggins burst in, bearing a heavy trunk. 'Here I am, folks, on time again. An' guess who my passenger is – the purtiest gal in Arizone-ee!'

Sally Roberts, in a blue check travelling costume, hobbled in tight around her ankles, bustled in, and bustle it was, for she had her backside accentuated beneath her skirt by the latest Parisian fashion, a 'bum-cooler' or bustle. She had a little blue hat, with a veil, on top of her blonde and now ringleted hair. She gave them all a dazzling smile, posing with her parasol.

'Jeez,' Luke drawled with awe. 'I hardly recognized you, Sal.'

'You told me to buy a new honeymoon outfit so here it is. What's wrong, honey?'

'Nuthin'. But we ain't married yet.'

'There's no time like now, Luke. Mr Harris is here.' Ruby grinned as she saw Luke's confusion.

'He'll write the certificate. Go get the judge. He'll bang his gavel on the bar and that's all there is to it.'

'I ain't the marryin' kind, Ruby,' Luke muttered. 'Maybe this ain't a good idea. Why do I get the feelin' I'm bein' railroaded into it?'

'Come on, pardner. Cheer up. It's your wedding day. I'll go dig out some more crates of that French champagne. This is going to be a night to remember. Never mind, Luke' – she gave him a nudge with her elbow – 'you ever get a bit tired of the old ball and chain, you can always come and see Ruby. Or Isabella. Or the widow. Hey, man, why don't you become a Mormon?'

'It ain't funny,' he said, glumly.

But when the judge pronounced them man and wife he saw the funny side, squeezed Sally to him, and gave her a resounding kiss. Fiddle, harp, flute, squeezebox and Indian drum thrummed out their discordant melodies, and everybody did what they liked best, to doze-ee-do and promenade, whooping like Apaches as whiskey and champagne was sloshed in profusion. In between swinging his little honey in the Texan two-step Luke vaguely remembered getting up on the bar and telling everybody that he might stand as sheriff after all, and that anybody, Latino, Indian, or American, who had been swindled out of their land by his twin brother had only to apply to him and they could have it back gratis. 'This is goin' to be a decent town to live, to bring your kids up in from now on. You folks back me and I'll back you,' he yelled. 'In the morning me and Sal are settin' out on the stage for Tooh-sohn and Yuma. We'll take the steamboat up to San Francisco and see y'll back here in two months' time. But tonight we got some catchin' up to do.'

At that he swept Sally off her feet and carried her up to the honeymoon suite. On the landing he paused and shouted, 'I been thinking of naming this place Jonestown, but hell, it don't have the same ring as Cameron. So we'll let it stay as it is for old times sake.'